Timothy Coop, Henry Exley

A Trip Around the World

Timothy Coop, Henry Exley

A Trip Around the World

ISBN/EAN: 9783337144814

Printed in Europe, USA, Canada, Australia, Japan

Cover: Foto ©Andreas Hilbeck / pixelio.de

More available books at **www.hansebooks.com**

TIMOTHY COOP.

A TRIP

AROUND THE WORLD

A SERIES OF LETTERS

BY

TIMOTHY COOP AND HENRY EXLEY

With Twelve Albertype Plates

CINCINNATI

H. C. HALL & COMPANY, 180 ELM STREET

1882

Electrotyped at
FRANKLIN TYPE FOUNDRY,
Cincinnati, O.

PREFACE.

In sending forth from the press books and letters of travel, a very common statement is made — that the letters, etc., were not written or intended for the public eye, but only for the enjoyment of the immediate friends of their writers. Without being able to say just the same thing, this much, however, is literally correct, that neither of the writers of the letters here sent forth, had any idea whatever of publishing a book; scarcely, indeed, of publishing even a series of letters for the *Christian Standard*, in which they appeared. As they were written and sent off from different parts of the world; it was always with the fear that they were very far below, in their interest and worth, the requirements of such a paper. It is no small gratification to the writers, to find that, where they had feared so much, the readers of the letters have enjoyed so much ; and so many of them express a wish to possess them in a permanent form. Such as they are, we send them to the churches, greeting, but with much fear and diffidence. Did the readers know the real difficulties under which they were written, more than common allowance and indulgence would be granted for whatever faults may mar the letters, either in matter or style.

We confess to a little real satisfaction, in thinking that, with all their blemishes, they are a kind of *pioneer trip 'round the world* series of letters, amongst us a people, so far as we have any knowledge of the matter.

In every case where we have had to draw upon other sources than our own, on matters of realest interest, but often entirely beyond our own observation, we have drawn from the best and most reliable; in the first place, that we might ourselves know something about the strange lands we were visiting, and so be enabled to gather instruction and pleasure at every point of our journey — without which it could not be done, except to a small extent; and in the next place, if we published any letters whatever, the readers of them should share in the feast. For many interesting items about missionaries and their work, such authorities as Revs. Taplin, Ingliss, Reid and Williams, all toilers in the fields of the world; for facts concerning the various lands we visited, the natives, natural history, and kindred matters, Miss Bird, Canon Tristram, Harcus, the Historian of South Australia, Boswick, F. R. G. S., Historian of the Tasmanians, have been our sources; besides which, a constant lookout was kept for everything that might keep us abreast with what was transpiring around us, as we moved from city to city, and from land to land.

In suffering this little book to go forth amongst the brethren, to whom we send it with Christian greetings, we send it in the hope that it will help, under the Divine blessing, to awaken more interest in the work of missions, and to bring together, as never in the past, all who are pleading for a full return to the right ways of the Lord, into closer bonds of brotherhood, warmer sympathies, and world-wide united activities.

If our small contribution in these letters, shall help in even a very small degree, to accomplish this, our long journey will not have been altogether in vain. It is our abiding conviction that the gospel calls on us, and our assumed position demands of us, that we seek the extension of the Redeemer's kingdom; not only where Christ is preached, and where His gospel needs to be freed from the traditions of men, but in the regions beyond us, and where dark habitations of cruelty still abound, and teeming millions still sit in the darkness, and in the valley of the shadow of death, and where no light is.

We are sure that if all the churches in America could have seen what we saw — the many large churches, and so intensely alive to the interests of the kingdom of our common Lord, they could not help but thank God and take courage. It appeared to us that the churches of Australia have, for their years and opportunities, gone beyond what their brethren elsewhere have done.

With many fears, and some hopes, we venture to send forth these letters to the churches, hoping that they may prove to be at least one link in a golden chain of Christian love and world-wide sympathy, that shall help to bind them all together.

We pray that a rich blessing from the great Lord of the harvest may rest upon them, and cause them to minister to the joys of His people, and the salvation of men.

T. Coop, H. Exley.

CONTENTS.

(vii)

A TRIP AROUND THE WORLD.

LETTER I.

FROM OMAHA TO THE PACIFIC.

On Friday evening, September 17, 1880, I received a telegram from Bro. Coop, proposing to me what amounted to a trip around the world — not for pleasure and health only, but to take a brief survey of whatever of mission work might fall in our path on the journey.

In the true spirit of missions, my dear wife at once consented to give me up, and at no small cost to herself of heavy care, hard work and real privation. A deluge, almost, of rain fell during the night, making it doubtful if it would be possible to drive over the seven miles intervening between me and the Union Pacific depot at Lincoln.

On Saturday morning, at five o'clock, gathering my dear ones around me, and all kneeling in prayer, commending them to the Father's care, I left home once more, "not knowing what should befall me."

My son drove me to Lincoln, the water on my own farm running over the bottom of the buggy. Reaching Omaha at 12:15, I found Bro. Coop quietly enjoying a lunch in the sleeping-car. The moment he saw me he was on his feet and off to the ticket-office. In purchasing a ticket to San Francisco, one of those curious mistakes occurred which involve several others. In the hurry of the moment, whilst Bro. Coop paid down the money for a first-class ticket, the agent, by mistake, gave him an *emigrant* ticket! Neither of them observed the mistake. Going then to the office of the Pullman Sleeping Car Company, the agent, without observing the mistake, sold him a ticket for the sleeping-car, handing both tickets to me. I did not observe the mistake either, and showing them both to the keeper of the car, he also failed to see it, and passed me in. By and by the train moved off, and the conductor examined the ticket and checked it off—and he did not discover the mistake either.

On Lord's day afternoon, when a new conductor came on the train, the moment he saw the ticket, he said: "I can not honor that ticket!" Then the mistake was apparent enough. A telegram was sent to Omaha from the next station to ask about the mistake, and on Monday evening we received an answer correcting it. The conductors were all exceedingly courteous in the whole matter.

At most of the hotels on the whole line from Omaha to San Francisco, the meals provided are very

much worse in quality, and the charge for them just
as high, as in the superbly splendid Palace Hotel of
San Francisco. Some of them are not much better
than places designed to give very poor meals at very
extortionate charges.

After leaving Omaha, we were astonished at the
universally desolate aspect of the whole country. It
requires more than the average stock of love of country to see anything beautiful for very many hundreds
of miles. A sail up the river Clyde, in Scotland, or
the river Hudson, in New York State, will furnish
more to delight the eye and satisfy a love of the
beautiful than the whole distance from Omaha to San
Francisco. Desolation holds supreme dominion.

Finding that we could spend one night and most of
one day in Salt Lake City, and still be in time, with
nearly two days to spare, to spend in San Francisco
before embarking for Australia, we broke our journey
at Reno, and taking the cars on the Utah Central
Pacific at 7 P. M., in about two hours we were in the
far-famed city of Mormons and polygamy. Of course
our curiosity was intensely alive, and we did our best
to gratify it in the few hours at our disposal. We
put up at the Walker House, the best hotel in the
city. Whether the owners are Mormons, we did not
clearly ascertain.

The city itself is most admirably laid out. The
streets, miles in length, are 132 feet wide, including
the very ample sidewalks. Most of the streets are
planted on either side with a splendid line of the

locust tree, which here did not seem to be so subject
to the ravages of the borer as in Iowa or Wisconsin. The shade afforded by them is very agreeable,
whilst underneath each line of shade trees, close to
the curb of the sidewalk, there runs a fine stream of
clear, cool water, brought from the mountains. Of
course, Salt Lake being to the Mormon the Zion of
the last days, it is very natural that he should call at
least one of the rivers of the valley, the Jordan.
Located on one of the banks of the Utah Jordan, it
is said, resides an apostle or bishop of the saints, who
has the rare faculty of ruling about eleven wives! It
is, however, waggishly suggested that he does sometimes sing in plaintive tone —

"On Jordan's stormy banks I stand," etc.

As we were nearing Salt Lake City on the cars, we
became aware that we were in close proximity to both
a Mormon apostle and a bishop. We dropped into
conversation with them, and were not a little surprised to find the apostle as agreeably communicative
as one could desire. He pointed out objects of interest on the road, told us he had been to England, and
had held "conferences" in nearly every county in the
kingdom. He told us that if we were at the Temple
about 11 o'clock on the next day, he would introduce
us to the President of the church.

After reaching our hotel, and taking supper, we
had a stroll through one or two of the streets of Salt
Lake City. The quiet and order are very noticeable.

At least three-fourths of the entire population are Mormons, although the Protestant Episcopalians, the Methodists, Catholics, Presbyterians and Congregationalists, have each a church edifice in the city. Every business man to whom we spoke was a Mormon — excepting one or two — and apparently, most earnestly so. They were all, without exception, ready at once to enter upon a defense of the system, and like men who had entire faith in it. We were not a little surprised to find that in not one of them, with whom we conversed, was there even a shade of timidity, but in all a quiet, earnest, fearless readiness to avow their faith and defend it. Stepping into the street-cars, in which were three gentleman besides ourselves, we entered into conversation with them, apparently all strangers to each other, and found they were all Mormons. The eldest of them, in answer to our questions, told us that polygamy was not an institution for the richer Mormons only, but for the poorer ones also, and that great numbers of workingmen had more than one wife. This man was a Scotchman; told us he was married, had one wife and five children, but that his wife often pressed it upon him to take a second wife! His love for her, however, was so supreme, that he would not do so, lest, although she strongly desired it herself, he should grieve her by so doing! It was a strange thing to hear a Scotchman calmly enter into reasons in defense of the system. Every man to whom we spoke — and we spoke to many — answered our questions on the matter, like men who believed it to be a divine institution, reëstablished by direct revelation in these latter days. Another, with whom we entered into conversation, told us he was from Denmark, formerly fire-works maker to the King of Denmark. He said, in reply to our questions, that all his expectations in coming to Utah had been more than realized. All of them, when asked if they did not expect the General Government would put polygamy down, answered, "Never." Another, a tradesman, and one of the "Seventy," said to us, "Do you think, if I did not know that this was of God, that at the call of the church, I would leave my family and business, and without scrip or purse go on a mission to Europe?" He was, perhaps, 36 years of age, and had been on such a mission. He informed us that about three companies of Mormons, of about 400 each, had arrived at Salt Lake City, and that another company of about the same number was expected in a few days, and all of whom they had distributed, or would in two or three days, amongst their numbers, so that hardly one could be seen about the city in a day after their arrival. It is evident to almost the blindest observer, that apart from the religious infatuation which has drawn them together, the most consummate business skill enters into everything they do.

We visited the vast establishment called Zion Co-operative Mercantile Institution, all over which we were shown with the utmost readiness and courtesy. It is 330 feet long, by 99 in breadth, and filled from

HENRY KEELY.

basement to topmost room with such an array of mer-
chandise as the finest mercantile establishment in
Christendom might be proud of.

After this we went to visit the Tabernacle, and the
Temple now in course of erection. One of the Mormon officials most courteously conducted us to the
great Tabernacle, in the Temple Block. It is 233
by 133 feet, inside measurement, and consists simply
of one great roof, supported by 46 parallelogram pillars of red sandstone, and springs with a single stride
from side to side and from end to end. It is ellipti-
cal in form, and from ceiling to floor is 70 feet. It
has a seating capacity of 13,452, and at their gatherings it is often filled in every part. Perhaps there is
hardly a building in the world, of equal capacity,
more perfect in its acoustics than this. Good ears
can hear a pin drop, from the farthest part of it. Bro.
Coop stood in the place of the speaker, near the great
organ, and Bro. Exley went to the farthest point
away from him, in the gallery, and repeated, in a
low, conversational tone,

"Rock of ages, cleft for me," etc.

Coop could hear every word, whilst Exley could hear
him saying, "Slower." It boasts of possessing the
second largest organ in America (some say the *third*).
When it was constructed it was the largest that had
been built in America, and built by Utah artificers and
from material obtained in the Territory. The pipes
number nearly 3,000, the largest being 32 feet long

2

and 2 feet square on the inside. The entire structure is 58 feet to the top of the great towers, 33 feet deep, and 30 feet wide. Four men are required to work the blowers.

The building has 20 doors, all opening outward, and nearly all 9 feet wide, and so arranged that the vast building can be emptied in one and a half minutes.

The Temple, in course of erection, is a marvelous structure, and very imposing in appearance. Its walls are 9 feet 9 inches thick. Its corner-stone was laid April 6, 1853, and the building is now about 55 feet above the foundation. It has already cost over $3,000,000, and is expected to cost altogether some ten or twelve millions.

After this we went to the private office of President Taylor. Several clerks were busily employed, and a constant stream of men and women, on business of one kind or another, were passing in and out. We observed on the walls of the office several *playbills* of different kinds, advertising the very *mundane* tastes of these dwellers in the Utah Zion. After waiting a little, we were ushered, by Apostle Richards, into the presence of the President of all the Mormons — Apostle and President Jno. Taylor. He is a large man, well advanced in years, and quite imposing in appearance. We announced ourselves as travelers in search of information, especially on religious matters, and said we should be happy to receive any information he could give us. He received us

quite kindly, and at once entered into conversation
very freely. We asked him what proportion other
religious denominations in the city bore to that of the
Mormons. He said that he did not know very well
— that, in fact, he did not much trouble himself
about them. He informed us that the vast Temple
was being built out of the tithes and free-will offerings of the people, and that if the offerings were
abundant, it would be completed in about five years;
or it might be ten or even twenty years. He said
they gave all denominations welcome, and that his
principle was, that all should have full liberty to
carry out their convictions. We asked, " How many
preachers have you now engaged in foreign fields?"
He replied, " I do not exactly know, but we have a
great many, and a great many who are ready to go
when called upon." When asked how those preachers were sustained, he said that they went out without
scrip or purse, and were self-sustaining, and that they
had a large number ready to go on these terms!
When asked how fast they were increasing, his reply
was, " Rapidly." We asked, " From what nation-
ality do you receive most?" and his answer was, " I
think Scandinavia, and then Great Britain — mainly
Welsh — but very few from Ireland." They had also
many from the nations of Northern Europe. At this
point we thought we had occupied quite a reasonable
amount of time, and after thanking him for his kindness in so readily answering our questions, and after
an introduction to Joseph F. Smith, an apostle, and a

nephew of Joseph Smith, the founder of the system,
we withdrew. During the interview we learned from
Mr. Taylor, that they had 77 quorums, of 70 elders
each, and all of them ready to go and preach at the
church's bidding. One thing, omitted in writing
about the Great Tabernacle, is itself a noticeable
thing. On the left-hand side of the great organ is a
large collection of sage-brush, with small sun-flowers,
and one small pine tree, and on a large calico strip,
the figures 1847. This symbolizes that when the
Mormons came to Utah, in that year, they found not a
single blade of grass in the region; nothing but sage-
brush, sunflowers and pine trees. On the right-hand
side of the organ were sage-brush, sunflowers and
every variety of flowers, to indicate that they had
made the wilderness to blossom as the rose; and
amongst them all, in great figures, 1880. We came
away deeply impressed with the fact, that "organiza-
tion," thorough, systematic, and on the best business
plans, was at the root of all their success. We wondered what grand results for Christ and the world
would be accomplished by our brethren, if but a similar spirit filled them, and similar common sense and
business-like plans and methods could find a place
among us.

We left Utah's wonderful city at 3:30 P. M., Sept.
22, for Ogden, where again we set our faces west-
ward. In the cars again, we found, on entering into
conversation, Mormons were around us, and, as usual,
apparently most firm believers in the entire system.

(If I am not mistaken, as I think of it at this moment, this same President Taylor had a discussion at Boulogne-sur-mer, with some Protestant preacher, nearly forty years ago, and in it he denied the polygamous practices of the Mormons. I had a copy of that debate, and at the same time some published "revelations" on the subject, and in debate with a Salt Lake City elder in my native town, nearly thirty years ago, read from both, and with such effect that for nearly two years after no Mormon ever preached openly again in that town. I am reminded of this, as I think Mr. Taylor told us he had been in Europe. — EXLEY.)

We reached in safety San Francisco, Thursday evening, Sept. 23. When, as we were seeking our way to the entrance to cross on the ferry, a gentleman, hearing us asking the way, said: "You are English, are you not?" Bro. Exley replied, "Yes; and so are you, are you not?" "Yes." "From what part?" "Wakefield." Bro. Exley, grasping the man's hand, said, "So am I. Let me look at your face;" and after a close scrutiny, exclaimed, as he shook hands in a very warm fashion, and heartily laughing, "Why! it's Joe Moore! The last time I saw you was in Bradford, when I held that public debate with David Lighthowler, one of Mr. Joseph Barker's friends and followers." Mr. Moore said: "That is thirty-two years since. I was then a skeptic —a socialist of the Robert Owenites. I am now a Methodist."

We went to the Grand Hotel, and the first business attended to, was to look in the city directory, to see if there was a Christian Church. We found that there was, copied names and addresses of officers, and dispatched postal cards; and next evening Bros. H. H. Luse and McCollough waited upon us. We asked as to the condition of the cause in California, and were rejoiced to hear that a Woman's Board of Missions had been formed, and that the late State Meeting was the best ever held in the State. In San Francisco city we learned that there were about seventy members, and that Bro. McCollough was engaged as their preacher. He seems confident of success. We heard many reasons for the backward condition of the cause in California, one of which was the influence of a certain anti-mission paper; another, that some churches had almost been talked to death by an unhappy kind of "mutual teaching;" another reason was strife about the organ.

A curious settling of the organ question came to our knowledge. It seems that, in order to bring about a revival of the cause in California, it was proposed to send for Knowles Shaw. This brought up the item that he would have good music and singing; when the question was asked, "What is meant by good music?" The reply was, "An organ." Some at once wished to write to Knowles Shaw not to come. One brother then said, "As this organ question has been troubling us for a long time, I now propose that we settle that question by buying an organ." This was carried, an organ bought, and that question "sound-ly" settled.

On Saturday, Sept. 25, we took lunch at Bro. Luse's, in company with his very affable and courteous lady, and Bros. McCollough and Sturgess. After lunch, and conversation concerning the cause of the Master, Bro. Exley sat at the organ, Bro. Luse played the violin, and we all sang—

"I am so glad that Jesus loves me;"

after which we all knelt before the mercy-seat, and commended each other to the care of Him who made the sea, and the dry land also. We were then driven down to the vessel—the Zealandia—and in about two minutes after we were on board we stood clear of the shore, bound for New Zealand and Australia, and perhaps around the world.

At this point we close, as we expect to meet a vessel and send on with it our mail. We shall probably write again from Honolulu—certainly from New Zealand, where we expect to meet with Bro. Caleb Wallis, son of the late lamented James Wallis, of Nottingham, England, a gentleman on board giving us his address. T. COOP, H. EXLEY.

LETTER II.

OUR last letter was put into the Purser's hands two days before we reached Honolulu, supposing it would be transmitted to you by the mail-steamer we were expecting to meet; but, as we never saw it, the letter would be carried on to Honolulu, and there wait for the next mail-steamer. Owing to our haste to have it ready, it was likely a very disjointed letter.

We reached Honolulu, Sandwich Islands, on Saturday evening, Oct. 2, about 9 o'clock. We remained there until 11:20 Lord's day morning. Taking advantage of the time, we went on shore directly after breakfast, to see and learn what we could, in some three hours, at most, at our disposal. It was with real delight we stepped on shore and went into the city of Honolulu. Everything was so new, so strange, so beautiful. Some one has called the Sandwich Islands the "Paradise of the Pacific." There is said to be no local disease of any kind, or periodic sickness. The heat of summer is not oppressive, and the winters, if winter is at all applicable to such a country, are never cold! It was October when we went ashore at Honolulu, and the delightful warmth, the light, breezy air, and the strange and wonderful

(24)

growths of the feathered cocoanut—tall, beautiful,
and with great numbers of the fruit hanging upon
them — bananas, with their clusters of bananas, umbrella-trees, palm trees, and other tropical growths —
made us feel we were where all the conditions of life
are wonderfully unlike anything within the range of
our experience before. The very waters of the sea
surrounding these islands are an indescribable blue,
and the "mist upon the mountains" — mountains that
have been rocked and split and torn by earthquakes,
or have themselves belched out rivers of lava and
fire.— throws the charm of mystery over everything.

We went walking along several streets in the main
business part of the city. There are large numbers
of Chinese, and most that we saw, and we saw many,
seemed clean, tidy and wide-awake. We did not
learn if they had a "Joss" house, but we saw their
theater, and judging from a hasty outside view of it,
it seemed to be larger than any church building in the
city. They seemed to have a large number of shops,
and well crowded together. The dark-skinned Honolulans seemed a very quiet, cheerful, and very bright-
eyed people. Their eyes and teeth are unquestion-
ably beautiful. The movements of the younger
women are very graceful — nothing angular about
them. They all seem to love finery in dress. Most
of the women, no matter how well dressed otherwise,
seemed to be without shoes and stockings. All wore
a long, robe-like dress, and unconfined at the waist.
One rather elderly lady, dressed in a magnificent

crimson silk dress, attracted our notice by repeatedly stopping to so arrange her dress that the most of it could be seen, and also her spotlessly white underskirt at the same time.

When tired of walking, we hired a carriage, and were driven around the city by a native Honolulan — a city resting amidst cocoa-nuts, bananas, umbrella-trees, oranges, and passion-flowers. As we passed through the hospital grounds, we were almost horrified to find ourselves in such close proximity to leprosy. One man seemed to have no mouth, and the face of another was awful to look upon. Leprosy is doing a fearfully destructive work among the natives. It is called the "Chinese leprosy," but is attributable to quite other causes than climate or local disease or influence.

We visited the Congregational Church, in which the royal family worship — a large, substantial building — and the Roman Catholic Church, also very large, and very finely decorated with paintings. They have evidently a firm footing among the Honolulans. We also visited the Episcopalian Church, also large and substantial. The Episcopalians — of whom some one has written, that they plant a mission only where others have been before them — have the idea that they are called to some great work here, which others can not do so well as they. In a recent report of their work there, they thus discourse:

"The sumptuous Cathedral has not risen many inches above the ground, and the fund for its erection is at a standstill, if it be not exhausted. But the spiritual temple is growing, and the bishop, so far from being disheartened, declares that every day is opening out fresh opportunities for the mission — that the religion which the islanders received from the descendants of the pilgrim fathers, has lost its power, and that unless the people for whom the English Church twenty years ago professed so ardent a sympathy, are to fall a prey to emissaries from Utah, or to be drawn into the Church of Rome, his own hands must be strengthened. It is, in one aspect, a discouraging story the bishop has to tell, but it is gratifying to know that the Society's aid has saved an interesting mission from extinction, and the mother church from the full weight of reproach."

The future of religion in Honolulu may prove an extremely interesting study. We visited the Pacific Mission station, in the hope of learning any interesting particulars about missionary matters, but found no one there, as it appeared to be wholly abandoned to plasterers, etc., who were entirely rehabilitating it. The king's palace is a splendid building, and so is the block of buildings occupied by the government. We passed through the grounds occupied by the late Queen-Mother. She was to be buried the day of our visit. There was a very solid, broad *slide*, built from the ground up to the second story of her residence, down which the coffin was to be passed to the carriage to receive it. The weight of the coffin was said to be 12,000 pounds. A large number of passengers signed a request to the captain of our ship, to remain a few hours longer, that we might witness the funeral. He was unable to gratify us, and so, after we had exhausted our time, we went on board again. For fully

half an hour before sailing, we amused ourselves
watching a number of dark-skinned Honolulan boys,
who came swimming around the ship, and apparently
as much at home in the sea as ducks in a pond. A
goodly number of small pieces of silver were thrown
into the water, with as much force as possible; but
long before any piece could reach the bottom, these
little fellows, at once plunging down, heels over head,
had caught it, and as soon as the lucky one came to
the surface, he opened his hand, and holding it up between his thumb and fingers, put it into his mouth,
and was ready for another dive.

Salt water seems to have no influence on their eyes,
as they dive down with them wide open, and do n't
rub them when they come to the surface.

Since Capt. Cook discovered these Islands, in 1778,
very great changes have taken place. The inhabitants were then all idolaters, but not cannibals. It
may be, however, that there have been one or two exceptions to this. It was here Capt. Cook was murdered, and a monument has been erected to com-
memorate the catastrophe. It was not, however,
until 1819, that the inhabitants voluntarily threw
away their idols, and renounced idolatry; and not
until 1837, or nearly forty years after, that they manifested any intense interest in the Christian religion.
In 1835, Rev. Titus Coan, Congregationalist, entered
upon his work in these islands, as a missionary, prior
to which Mr. and Mrs. Lyman had for some years
been laboring, and evidently the good seed which

they had sown, had not been lost. On the first Lord's day in July, 1838, 2,400 persons, all of whom had been idolaters, were admitted to the Lord's table; and assuredly it was a wonderful gathering. Amongst them, "the old and decrepid, the lame, the blind, the maimed, the withered, the paralytic, and those afflicted with divers diseases and torments — some with their noses, lips and limbs consumed, with features destroyed, figures depraved and loathsome — these came hobbling along on their staves, or were borne by others, to the table of the Lord;" among them, the hoary priest of idolatry, with his hands but recently washed from the blood of human victims, together with thieves, idolaters, and mothers whose hands had reeked with the blood of their own children. From 1837, to 1841 or 1842, a great religious wave seems to have swept over these Islands, when even young people ran up into the mountains to carry the good news of the love of God to their benighted friends. They spoke of the good life to come to the old and sick, and of the "endless life of Jesus," as the most joyful news they had ever heard; as they said, "breaking upon them like light in the morning." "Will my spirit never die? and will this poor body live again?" exclaimed one old chieftess. Then there were only two preachers to 15,000 people; but the people were so eager to hear, that the sick and infirm were brought on litters, or carried on the backs of men — and some even crawled on their hands and knees, or any way they could, to the path over which

the missionary had to pass, that they might hear of
the good news, and saying, "If we die, let us die in
the light!"

The Islands are now Christian, and have all the
appliances of a well ordered kingdom, whilst their
king is a thoroughly well educated Christian gentleman. As evidence of the reality of the conversion of
these interesting people, it is stated that they have
contributed, since their renunciation of idolatry, some
hundreds of thousands of dollars, for missions. Mr.
Coan's congregation alone contributes more than
$1,200 yearly, for the work of foreign missions, and
twelve of its members have gone as missionaries to
the Isles of Southern Polynesia. Mr. Coan has himself admitted nearly 12,000 people into the church.
One very impressive testimony to the saving power of
the gospel, is given by Miss Bird, in her book on the
Sandwich Islands. The high-priest of the crater of
Kilauea, was considered a very awful personage.
This particular one was 6 feet 5 inches in hight, and
his sister, almost as tall, was coördinate with him in
authority. His chief business was to keep Pélé, the
goddess of the crater, appeased. He lived on the
shore, but often went up to Kilauea with sacrifices.
If any victim was demanded, he had only to point to
the native, and the unfortunate victim was at once
strangled. He was not only the embodiment of
heathen idolatry, but of heathen crime also. Robbery
was his pastime, and his temper was so fierce and un-
curbed, that no native dared to even tread on his

shadow. More than once he had killed a man for the sake of food and clothing not worth 50 cents. He was a thoroughly wicked savage. Curiosity attracted him to one of the mission meetings, and this bad giant fell under the power of the gospel whose strange influence was transforming thousands of his countrymen into new men. He said, " I have been deceived, and I have deceived others. I have lived in darkness, and did not know the true God. I worshiped what was no God; I renounce it all. The true God has come, and I will henceforth cleave to Him, and I will be his son." His sister, soon after, also fell under the same redeeming power, and both became truly Christian, and became loving and gentle as little children, and both, at last, at more than seventy years of age, passed peacefully away in the faith of Jesus. Of other things, more in our next.

Since writing the last letter, Bro. Exley has been very ill, and is now not nearly strong. Time is done, and this must be posted now, or a month may perhaps be lost. T. COOP, H. EXLEY.

AUCKLAND, New Zealand, Nov. 8, 1880.

LETTER III.

Our last letter was hurriedly finished at Papakura, in the house of Bro. Caleb Wallis, some twenty miles from Auckland, New Zealand. He is a right noble representative of his father, the late and much lamented James Wallis, editor of the British *Millennial Harbinger*, England. This letter we begin in the home of Bro. Grey, Wellington, situated at the extreme south of the North Island, and from whence we to-day sail for Christ Church, on the South Island.

It was a regret to us that our time did not allow us to visit the still active volcanoes of the Sandwich Islands, concerning which the most thrilling accounts have been written from time to time. The crater of the volcano Kilauea, which has a hight of 8,000 feet, nearly, is said to have the appearance of a great pit on a rolling plain; but such a pit! It is nine miles in circumference. Its depth is from 800 to 1100 feet, according as the molten sea below is at ebb or flood. The Hawaiians call it the Hate-maw-maw, or House of everlasting fire, and in Hawaiian mythology it is the abode of the dreaded Goddess Pélé. Here is a fiery sea, whose waves are never weary. Its area is six

(32)

square miles, showing signs of volcanic action over almost its whole extent. The movement of this vast, fiery sea, is nearly always from the sides to the center, but the movement of the center itself, appears to be independent, and always takes a southerly direction. The following description, by Miss Bird, published in 1876, is so graphic, that for the sake of many young readers, who may not see her book, it will not be unacceptable :

"It is the most unutterable of wonderful things. It is indescribable, unimaginable, a sight to remember forever — a sight which at once took possession of every faculty of sense and soul, removing one altogether out of the region of earthly life. Here was the real "bottomless pit," the "fire which is not quenched, the place of hell," "the place of fire and brimstone," "everlasting burnings," the "fiery sea whose waves are never weary." There were groanings, rumblings, and detonations; rushings, hissings, and splashings, and the crashing sound of breakers on the coast; but it was the surging of fiery waves upon a fiery shore. Now it seemed furious, demoniacal, as if no power on earth could hinder it; then playful and sportive: then, for a second, languid, but only because it was accumulating fresh force. On our arrival, eleven fire-fountains were playing joyously around the lake, and sometimes six of the nearest ran together in the center, to go wallowing down in one vortex, from which they reappeared, bulging upwards till they formed a huge cone thirty feet high, and which plunged down in whirlpools, only to reappear in exactly the previous number of fountains in different parts of the lake, high leaping, raging and flinging themselves upwards. Sometimes the whole lake, abandoning its usual centripetal motion, as if impelled southwards, took the form of mighty waves, and

3

surging heavily against the partial barrier, with a sound like
the Pacific surf, lashed, and tore, and covered it, and threw
itself over it in floods of living fire. It was all commotion,
confusion, force, terror, majesty, glory, mystery, and even
beauty. And the color! Molten metal has not that crimson
gleam, nor blood that living light. Had I not seen it, I
should never have known that such a color was possible.
Nearly the whole time the surgings of the lake, taking a
southerly course, broke on the bold, craggy cliffs, with a
tremendous noise, and throwing their gory spray to a hight
of fully 40 feet. Before we came away, a new impulse
seemed to seize the lava. The fire was thrown to a great
hight; the fountains and jets all wallowed together — new
ones appeared, and danced joyfully around the margin; then
converging toward the center, they merged into a glowing
mass, which upheaved itself pyramidally, and disappeared
with a mighty plunge. Then innumerable billows of fire
dashed themselves in the air, crashing and lashing, and the
lake, dividing itself, recoiled on either side; then hurling its
fires together, and rising as if by upheaval from below, it
surged over the temporary ruin it had formed, passing
downward in a slow, majestic flow, leaving the central surface, swaying and dashing in fruitless agony, as if sent on
some errand it had failed to accomplish."

A few years ago (1859) the volcano Mauna Loa
threw up fountains of fire nearly 400 feet in hight,
and of a nearly equal diameter. In 1868 terrors occurred which are without precedent in island history.
Earthquakes became nearly continuous, scarcely an
appreciable interval between them. The movements
of the earth were vertical, lateral, rotary and undul-
atory, producing nausea, vertigo and vomiting. The
crust of the earth rose and sank like the sea in a

storm. Rocks were rent, mountains fell, buildings and their contents were shattered, trees swayed like reeds, and animals were scared and ran about demented. Men thought the judgment day had come. Horses and their riders, and passengers on foot, were thrown violently to the ground. It seemed as if the rocky ribs of the mountains, and the granite walls and pillars of the earth, were broken up. From one of these volcanoes a pillar of fire 200 feet in diameter lifted itself for three weeks a thousand feet into the air, making night into day for a hundred miles 'round. From Mauna Loa, an eruption of fiery lava traveled in a straight line for forty miles — or sixty, including sinuosities; it was from one to three miles broad, and from five to two hundred feet deep, according to the contour of the mountain slopes over which it passed. It lasted for nearly thirteen months, pouring out a torrent of lava which covered about three hundred square miles of land, the contents of which were estimated at 38,000,000,000 cubic feet. In 1868, in the eruption which then took place, rocks weighing many tons were thrown from 500 to 1,000 feet into the air. Mr. Whiting, of Honolulu, who was near the spot, says that "from these great fountains there flowed to the sea a rapid stream of red lava, rolling, rushing and tumbling like a swollen river, bearing in its course large rocks, as it dashed down the precipices and the valley, into the sea, surging and roaring throughout its whole length like a cataract, with a power and a fury perfectly indescribable. It was

nothing else than a river of fire, from 200 to 800 feet
wide, and 20 feet deep, with a speed varying from ten
to twenty-five miles an hour." As one becomes acquainted with such stupendous facts as these, the significance and grandeur of the sacred question is
realized, " Who can understand the thunder of His
power?"

It was with reluctance we left these lands of marvel, of a simple, peaceful, and too rapidly diminishing
people, and set sail again on Lord's day, Oct. 3, at 11
A. M. Not much of special interest occurred to break
the sameness of our voyage, for days together. A
sail was hardly ever seen; a lazy turtle, too far off for
soup, and a large, black fish, of some kind, at a considerable distance, were about all the signs of life we
met, save numbers of flying fish, of which we saw
great numbers every day, one of them doing us the
special favor to fly over the bulwarks, making us
thus a flying visit. Its wings were about three-
fourths of its whole length.

On Lord's day, Oct. 10, we had Church of England service, in the morning at 10:30. In the afternoon, at 3 o'clock, Bro. Exley, having obtained per-
mission of the Captain, preached in the saloon, on
the "Divinity of Christ." The Episcopalian clergymen, of whom we had two on board, did not put in
an appearance at the meeting. Prior to the service,
the captain visited Bro. Exley in his state-room, and
said to him, "Mr. Exley, whilst personally I am glad
for you to preach, yet as these are Church of Eng-

land ships, it is hoped you will not say anything against the Church of England." Bro. Exley only said, "I know they are Church of England ships; but I do not believe in doing such work as you seem to fear. I am going to preach to them Christ, and think they will all rejoice in what I may say." The captain very kindly thanked him, and withdrew. In the evening there was Church of England service in the forward part of the vessel, and only some nine persons present all told. It was remarked over and over and over again, the littleness and sectarian spirit manifested in these gentlemen of the apostolic succession, and but few gave them their presence, whilst the discourse of Bro. Exley was the theme of general conversation, and evidently had done solid good. From this time, however, there came a serious change to Bro. Exley. Walking over the ice-smooth floor of the Palace Hotel at San Francisco, and with boots almost as smooth, he slipped, but did not fall, but in some way sprained his back in saving himself from falling. The sprain, though often felt, was thought to be of little consequence, and it was hoped that it would soon pass away. After preaching, however, perhaps from catching a little cold, the pain increased in intensity until he became almost helpless, and the weather changing for the worse, every lurching of the vessel was added torture, so that night and day it was continual suffering for the rest of voyage to Auckland, and a considerable portion of the intervening seven days, he was unable to walk alone.

We crossed the equator on Thursday, the 9th of
October. It was very amusing to stand at noon beneath the sun, and look at our shadows, all cuddled
up under our feet. On the 10th of October we
passed the Navigator Islands, and the Sunday Islands
on the 14th. It was exceedingly warm, and had it
not been for the canvas awning covering the whole
of the hurricane deck, 'it would have been very un-
comfortable. Our ship's company was every way
good — quite a number of tourists — one we took to
be a sleek Jesuit, ready to thrust the claims of his
church before one at every opportunity, "instant in
season and out of season," and almost as ready to be
quite angry and insolent when rather hard pressed.
Once, over the dinner-table, Bro. Exley asked him,
"Where is your home?" He blandly said, with a
smile, and his eyes half closed, as he pointed upward,
"Above." Bro. Exley then pleasantly said, "Well,
yes, I would hope so; but on the road, where is your
stopping-place?" At this he was a little taken aback,
and looked hard, but said nothing. Bro. Coop. with
a quiet emphasis, said, "I know I should not like to
stop long at one place on the road?" Our Catholic
friend saw in that a rather unpleasant reminder of his
possible retention, for a time, in purgatory, and so ate
the balance of his dinner in silence.

On Thursday, at midnight, Oct. 14, we passed at
once to Saturday, the 16th. We had no Friday. The
doctor visiting Bro. Exley, and a high churchman,
was asked a rather puzzling question : " Doctor, how

do you high church people manage, when crossing this region at the time of the year, to keep Good Friday?" Of course he had no answer. Our ship's steward was exceedingly kind, and to Bro. Exley he was almost as gentle as a brother.

On Lord's day, the 17th, we reached the city of Auckland, at noon, where, for two or three reasons, we determined to land and spend a little time. Bro. Exley was too ill to continue the journey — then we wanted to know if there was a church there, and to see how they were doing; and lastly, but not least, we wanted to see Bro. Caleb Wallis, of Papakura. We went on shore at 2:30 P. M., and were at once driven to the Star Hotel. A physician was at once sent for, as sought out by Bro. Coop, as Bro. Exley was unable to sit up. It was found that, in addition to the sprain in the back, the treatment of the ship's doctor had entirely stripped the skin from a large portion of the · side. This had to be healed before anything could be done for the back. Bro. Coop, as usual, went off to see and learn all about the churches, both of our brethren and others, and succeeded soon in finding a church of our brethren.

As this letter, however, is long enough, and not over interesting, all about these matters must be left for another letter.

On Monday, Bro. Carr, a lumber merchant, and old Bro. Rattray, an old sea captain, dropped in to see us; the latter had, a short time before, celebrated his golden wedding.

Also, there came to see us, a **Mr. George A. Brown,**
a Baptist minister, formerly of Lincoln, England,
a gentleman who is preaching in the Temperance
Hall, to large audiences, on Lord's day evenings.
He is doing solidly good work in weakening the
hold of sectarianism upon the people. Apart from
his advocacy of the doctrine of the destruction of the
wicked, he is doing precisely the work our people are
seeking to do. It would not, at present, be wise for
them to unite; but union may come, and will, if all
parties are governed by the right spirit.

On Friday, the 22nd, Bro. and sister McDermott,
having laarned of Bro. Exley's condition, insisted we
should move from the hotel to their house, so that he
could have as good nursing as if he were in his own
home. And certainly, if any proof were needed of
the precious influence of the gospel of Jesus, Bro.
and Sister McDermott and family are a splendid testimony. A more affectionate, well-ordered family, it
would be hard to imagine. He himself was born in
New Zealand, and with his father and mother has, in
past years, been in strange perils from the Maories.
She is from Ireland, and formerly a Roman Catholic, we understand, but is now a member of the Christian Church, as is her mother, formerly a Catholic
also. Their names and their home will always have a
place of affectionate remembrance in our hearts.

T. COOP, H. EXLEY.

WELLINGTON, New Zealand, Nov. 30, 1880.

LETTER IV.

As BEFORE intimated, on our arrival at Auckland, we found the whole city in considerable agitation, it being stirred up by the preaching of Mr. George A. Brown. He is a personal friend of Bro. J. B. Rotherham, and knows Bro. Delaunay, of Paris, quite well. The people in the colonies, for the most part, seem remarkably free from prejudice, so that, to an earnest and fearless proclaimer of the truth, there is much cause for encouragement. Bro. Coop soon found himself quite busy in the place — and several pleasant little things happened to him as he went up and down the city. He was frequently and suddenly accosted by some one who had either known him, or worked for him, or traded with him, in England.

For five weeks we stayed at Auckland, minus some ten days spent at Papakura, at Bro. Wallis's hospitable home. During this time Bro. Coop, very much with the view of drawing Mr. Brown and our brethren together, frequently *broke bread* with him and those affiliated with him. Mr. Brown's preaching is doing good work on the side of a purer faith, and our brethren repeatedly allowed him to use their baptistery. On the design of baptism he is thoroughly at one

(41)

with us.   Bro. Coop repeatedly assisted him on these occasions, baptizing for him, nine at one time, six at another, and some four or five at another, whilst Mr. Brown baptized also a still larger number.

To none of these meetings was Bro. Exley able to go, being at times unable to stand more than a few minutes.   Under the careful nursing of Sister Mc-Dermott, however, strength gradually returned, and whilst able to barely walk about, a few minutes at a time, he resolved to preach for the brethren a few times.   This he did, twice on the Lord's day, Oct. 31, speaking in the morning on "The Cross, the Throne and the Crown;" and in the evening, on "The Great Question of this Age."   It was pleasing to meet faces on this Lord's day, not seen before for seventeen years — Bro. and Sister Roebuck, from Camden Town, London, with many friends from there, and some from Manchester, who had heard Bro. Exley preach there many years ago.

After this, we went to Bro. Wallis's, at Papakura, who kindly met us at the depot with his conveyance. Bro. Exley had seen him but once or twice before, when it happened he preached in Huddersfield, nearly thirty years ago.   He had brought his little daughter with him, whom we knew at once, because of her close resemblance to Sister Black, of London, a sister of Bro. Wallis.   Here Bro. Exley preached five times, on various themes; some by request, such as "The Witness of the Spirit," "Eternal Life," "Jesus, the Son of God," and suchlike themes.   The

meetings were large, for a country place, and held in
the National School-room. There is a little church
here of somewhat over twenty members, and of a
superior class to some, gathered mainly by the labors
of Bro. Wallis. The family of Bro. and Sister Wallis, consisting of one son and three daughters, all
members of the church, except the little girl, is in
every way a model family. The Christian kindness, gentleness, wisdom and affection, which obtain
amongst them all, we have rarely seen equalled, and
never surpassed. Their unceasing efforts to have
Bro. Exley built up into strength again, and to make
us thoroughly at home, can not be overvalued. Indeed, had it not been for the care of Bro. and Sister
Wallis, and family, and of Bro. and Sister McDermott, and family, it is very doubtful if Bro. Exley
had been able for a long time to have done any work
again, or to have continued the journey. Surely it is
of such gentle and tender kindness as theirs, that the
Master has said, " Inasmuch as ye did it to one of the
least of these, my brethren, ye did it unto me;" and
it may be that it will be of just such deeds of pure
Christian love as these, that the " *Crown of Life*"
will be woven by the Master's hand in that day,
when it will show forth the nobleness of the life of
the wearer to whom it is given.

Whilst Bro. Exley was thus by day being nursed so
kindly, and trying to preach sometimes at night, Bro.
Coop was busy exploring the country with Bro. Wallis, and in various ways showing himself either a real

"sport," or a man equal to emergencies in awkward
situations. One day he and Bro. Wallis started on
horseback to the distant hills, and had the lucky misfortune to have his horse, after he had dismounted
and tied it up, break loose and take to the bush, and
he had to turn *bushranger*, or *bushwhacker*, in reality,
as also Bro. Wallis, to go in search of their scared
and runaway nags. It was something of a picture to
see a man sixty-four years of age, with face excite-
ment-flushed and eye flashing with merriment, and
himself apparently as vigorous as a young fellow of
thirty, enjoying the sport. At another time, going
off with his nephew, Mr. James Coop, a drive into
the country some twenty miles, and coming to a
stream, they there decided to "git out" and give the
animal a chance to drink. Having done this, the
horse took a sudden notion to plunge forward, but
not far enough to reach the other side, and — to their
great amazement and discomfort — it sank in water
and mud almost up to the neck. They had the nice
pastime of standing up to the arm-pits in the new
situation, trying to get it out; but having first to un-
harness the horse, which, being done, with a plunge
and a bound, flinging his companions right and left
still deeper, the horse got out, after which — what a
picture! If they had been "gold-washing" in a clay
pit, they might, perhaps, have looked as nice. Then
the buggy was so well embedded in the new situation,
that a span of horses had to be hitched on to get it
out. Altogether, they had a fine time of it. An-

other day, Bro. Coop, with others, went out in a boat
into the bay, a-fishing—and did what might have ex-
cited the envy of even good old Isaac Walton, the
prince of fisher-sportsmen. He not only out-did the
rest of the company in the success of his "catch,"
but, *mirabile dictu*, he actually caught a shark, which,
with the aid of the rest, he succeeded in getting into
the boat. This, however, they destroyed and flung
overboard again, without even securing its formidable
but beautiful teeth, as reminders of the sport. At
night he returned home, as wet as a sailor (do sailors
get wet in fishing?) and loaded with the day's spoils.

We had now been in and about Auckland for about
four weeks, Bro. Exley getting stronger all the time,
and by way of exercise, not being able to walk much
or ride much, determined to try and make amends by
preaching as often as he could. The doctor shook his
head, but "better rub than rust" was the motto, and
so, altogether, he preached at Papakura, five discourses, and at Auckland, eleven, on as many themes.
One Lord's day evening, in the hope of cultivating a
fraternal intercourse between our brethren and Mr.
Brown and those with him, Bro. Exley preached in
Temperance Hall, instead of Mr. Brown, on "The
Nobleness of Serving Christ." There was a very
large attendance. The sects are hard on Mr. Brown,
a sure sign that, whether he is right or wrong, they
are being greatly disturbed by his preaching. On the
last Lord's day in Auckland, Bro. Exley spoke in the
morning on "Precious Promises," and in the even-

ing on the "Ascension of Christ." At the close,
some ten young persons, from 13 to 17 years of age,
came forward and confessed the Saviour's name. On
Monday evening, he preached again on "The Three
Gracious Commands," and immediately after baptized twelve persons. After dismissing the meeting,
but before the congregation had begun to disperse, a
lady came forward, and in earnest tones said she was
thoroughly convinced of the truth, and desired to
yield obedience to the Saviour. Her confession was
most earnest, as well as clear, and a second time Bro.
Exley "went down into the water." No sooner had
he baptized this lady, and "come up out of the
water," than a third time he had again to go into the
bath, to baptize two others, thus baptizing fifteen persons that evening. Could we have remained a week
or two longer, no doubt a greater work could have
been done, as great seriousness appeared to rest upon
the people, evidently a work of grace. But we could
not stay. Our visit to the beautiful city of Auckland will not be soon forgotten by us, or by the
brethren. The memories of some of them will henceforth be a part of our lives, and a very precious part
indeed. The church at Auckland numbers about 140
members now, has four elders and three deacons,
with a Sunday-school of about sixty scholars. Prior
to our visit, the church had, in six years, had some
ninety-two additions, but none under sixteen years of
age. Bro. Coop, whenever he had opportunity, plead-
ed for the little ones, and, we hope, with good effect.

On Tuesday, the 23d of November, we bade farewell to Auckland, accompanied on the cars as far as Onehunga, by Bro. and Sister McDermott, and Sisters Carr and Stokes. Our vessel was soon under way, and faces known to us but for a few weeks, faded from our sight, but not to fade from memory in this life any more. The church at Auckland has no evangelist, and under such circumstances has done exceedingly well. The Lord make the church there a mighty power for good! Our vessel, the *Hawea*, was about 800 tons, and not being very large, although a first-rate vessel, she answered well to the motion of the waves, and severe sea-sickness was the lot of many of our passengers.

There is one pleasing feature among the colonists, which is too much lacking in the United States: they preserve, to a very large extent, the Maorie names. Hardly a place in the country, except the large seacoast cities, but what bears a Maorie name. So with the ships. One of the two we have sailed in since reaching Auckland, is named the " Hawea," and the other the " Rotomahana." On our arrival at Auckland, Bro. Coop busied himself in learning the religious status of different societies; finding himself in company with an Episcopalian clergyman, who was attending Convocation in the city, ascertained that the Episcopalians have no less than fifteen ordained Maories as clergymen. Yet we hear that the religion of the cross does not make much headway amongst the natives. Various reasons are assigned for this.

Some say, it is because the missionaries, for the most part, have managed to get hold of the best portion of their lands; others, that they have become possessed of a large portion of wealth, from the sale of their lands, and as a consequence have become enervated by it, averse to Christianity, and by their deteriorated habits are rapidly dwindling away. It is a great misfortune to them, and pity. They are a splendid race of people. All that we saw were, for the most part, finely proportioned, well dressed, and apparently very intelligent, both men and women. The married women are tattooed on the mouth, both upper and lower lips. Tattooing is, however, said to be abandoned now. Bro. Coop also made the acquaintance of the Baptist ministers, Webb and Jones. They have one good, strong church in Auckland, and two smaller, or branch-churches. They also have three Sunday-schools, and they are so careful in the training of their Sunday-school scholars, that they have baptized a large number of them, and have now a large class of from fourteen to sixteen years of age, under instruction, with a view to baptism. They have some baptized as young as nine years of age. All this is grand, and we write it here for brethren to see it, and learn a lesson or two from it, if possible. We learned that the chief Maorie, who had embraced Christianity from some influence or another, had been led to imagine himself a divinely commissioned leader, and to him large numbers of Maories look for instruction. He is exceedingly well versed

in the scriptures, but **has**, no doubt, embraced some
kind of spiritualism. **All this** makes it difficult **to**
spread a purer faith amongst **them**.

Before leaving Auckland, we had a long drive up a
winding pathway, to the top of Mount **Eden**, an extinct volcano. Bro. and Sister McDermott, and Bro.
Coop, with his nephew, all made the ascent. It commands a very wide area of land and sea, in its range
of vision. The cup, or hollow of the crater, is still
in perfect form. It is, perhaps, one-sixth of a mile
across. It is a singular fact that stones thrown, by
strong men, and with slings to help give force,
seem to fall at but a short distance from the men
flinging them. One of our company tried to throw
a stone, but without a sling, and it seemed to be
drawn down into the crater, at a short distance.

The entire region is of volcanic origin, and the
lava is still visible in places, over the whole distance
to the sea.

Leaving Auckland, we found the whole coast-line
of the country, with hardly the semblance of a break,
one continuous line of bold, lofty and very precipi-
tous mountains. This is the unbroken characteristic
of both North and South Islands, and all round about
them.

We passed New Plymouth, but did not go on
shore, as that could only be done by going in a small
boat, and through a very high and heavy surf. At
Nelson, however, we went on shore for a few hours,
and had a ride around.

4

The cities of New Zealand are exceedingly beautiful — better laid out, perhaps, than any city west of
the Mississippi.   Roads, side-paths, are built after .
the solid fashion in England.   Schools are many, and
built in the finest taste; and everything indicates a
people fully abreast with the best countries in the
world, whilst the mildness of the climate — ice being
in most places utterly unknown, and the summers
never excessively hot — and the wonderful cleanliness
of everything and everybody, make these islands
one of the most desirable homes on earth.   We tried
to find brethren at Nelson, but did not succeed; but,
instead, we found that the Plymouth Brethren had a
footing there, divided into " fast " and " loose " brethren.   Amongst a number of tracts, kindly given us,
quite characteristic of the teaching of these good
people, was one with the curious title, " The First-
ling of an Ass."   Surely, neither Moses nor Job
ever dreamed they would be thus honored, by having
their language used as proof that all men are *asses!*
Is there any truth in " evolution "?   The writer impressively says, " It is far easier to acknowledge that
we have acted *like* asses, than to acknowledge that we
are such."   With this Nelsonian piece of Plymouth
Brethrenism, we left the city, speculating whether we
were not also as Ephraim, " cakes unturned " — in
fact, baked a little too much on one side.

On Tuesday, the 27th, we landed at the port and
city of Wellington, where we were met by Bro. T. H. ·
Bates, evangelist, and several others, who had been

warned by telegram from Auckland, of our intended visit. Wellington is built on hills, and is a splendid city. The church here numbers about ninety members; of these only some nineteen were there when Bro. Maston settled among them, last February. He has done well. Bro. Bates was there on an exchange with Bro. Maston, who was at Christ Church in his place.

We were most kindly entertained by good Bro. and Sister Gray. He is one of the elders of the church. Bro. Coop addressed the church on Lord's day morning, on the "Church's Duty to the Young." The material of this church seems to be good. At night, Bro. Exley, in the same hall, addressed a crowded audience, on "God's Method of Salvation." The attention was intensely earnest, from the first sentence to the last. Two persons — a lady and a gentleman — came forward, and desired to consecrate all to Him who had died for them. Bro. Bates had baptized six the evening before our arrival. They have prayer-meeting and Bible-class, but no Sunday-school, not having yet the proper facilities. The church is in good order, with additions constantly, under the earnest labors of Bro. Maston, who has not only a fine field here, but a place in the hearts of the brethren.

Leaving Wellington on Monday, the 29th, we sailed in the Rotomahana, for Christ Church. Never have we seen such great, swelling waves, and billows of such immense sweep, but in mid-Atlantic, as met

us on emerging from the harbor and bay of Wellington. Our vessel, though large and of good beam,
literally groaned and plunged as we bravely breasted
them. Bro. Bates and wife accompanied us, as they
were leaving for Christ Church, that Bro. Maston
might return to his own field of labor. We arrived
at the port and city of Lyttleton next morning, and
were also met here by a number of brethren already
assembled to meet us and give Bro. and Sister Bates
welcome home. The city of Christ Church is some
six miles from Lyttleton, to reach which we have to
go by rail, passing under the immense hills by tun-
nel. "The rocks for the conies," but at Lyttleton
they are taken possession of by men. The church at
Christ Church numbers about 120, about two-thirds
of whom have been brought into the fold by the
labors of Bro. Bates. He is about to leave here for
Melbourne; the church will then be without help,
and the consequences can not be good. They have a
Sunday-school of about thirty scholars.

On Wednesday evening, the church had a tea-
meeting in the Odd Fellows' Hall, and, although it
was a wet evening, about 280 persons sat down to
tea. Afterward came singing, by a number of the
trained members of the church, and speeches by
Brethren Bates, Maston, Coop and Exley were made,
the latter of whom closed by singing them a song,

"The good we may do,"

to the great delight of all. A large number bade us

good-bye, and many, as Bro. Bates is likely to leave, expressed a strong desire for Bro. Exley to come and labor amongst them, as also was the case at Auckland and Papakura.

On Thursday, the 2nd of December, we bade adieu also to Christ Church. The city stands on an immense level plain, perhaps the finest farming region in New Zealand, and the whole region was given many years ago, by the government, to the Episcopalians, as was the region to the Presbyterians on which Dunedin stands. Then the plain was a *swamp*, but they have drained it, and it is now a garden, if there is one anywhere. The Episcopalians are now erecting a very large cathedral, the tower of which is already more than ninety feet high. Here Bro. Exley met with Bro. Peter Duncan, a brother who came to the acknowledgment of the truth some seventeen years ago, under his preaching at Long Grove, Iowa. This was one of the happiest little episodes of our journey. He is a substantial farmer at Okuku (pronounced Okookoo), some thirty miles from Christ Church. He assured us that, on good land in this region, it was a common thing to raise sixty bushels of wheat per acre, and from ten to twenty tons of potatoes — the wheat selling at four English shillings (ninety-six cents) per bushel. He told us that he realized thirteen pounds, or more than sixty dollars, per acre, for all his potatoes, the last season. On poorer lands the average of wheat is about twenty-two to twenty-five bushels per acre, and of potatoes, about eight tons. With facts like these, New Zealand will not be easily undersold in England by our Western producers.

The mail leaves this evening, and we close this, only saying that, leaving Christ Church yesterday, by our former boat, the "Hawea," after a very stormy passage of some twenty hours, we are now safely domiciled with Sister Stewart, at Dunedin. We are both moderately well, and as Bro. M. Green, the preacher here, is on a visit to the Melbourne Exhibition, we are both given to understand we must do his work on next Lord's day.   T. COOP, H. EXLEY.

LETTER V.

As YOU see from *date* and *place*, we are actually in far-off Australia. Hitherto the Lord has brought us in safety. After we left Christ Church, in New Zealand, Bro. Coop spent about one full week in Dunedin, and Bro. Exley about two. We were kindly and most hospitably entertained during our whole stay, at the house of Captain Stewart, one of the brethren, but who is now on a visit to his native Scotland, and also to England. He has the reputation of being a genuine disciple. His good lady, Sister Stewart, and family of four daughters and three sons, did all they could to make us at home and happy, and they succeeded well. Long will the memory of their loving kindness remain with us, as one of the most precious of all our acquisitions in New Zealand. There are two churches in Dunedin; one of about 450 members, the preacher for which church is Bro. Matthew W. Green, who appears to have done a good work there, and whose noble efforts against the deadly and destructive influence of "Spiritism" have secured him the esteem and good will of not a few in Dunedin. The second church numbers about sixty members, and very choice spirits, too, we gathered,

(55)

many of them are. They have at present no preacher, but, after hearing Bro. Exley preach some six or seven times in the "Tabernacle," in place of Bro. Green, who was on a trip to Australia, mainly for his health, the church meeting in the "Temperance Hall" sent him an official invitation and offer, exceedingly liberal and gratifying in themselves, and which, had circumstances favored, Bro. Exley would have accepted. He, however, left the matter open, so that, provided he could see his way clear to accept the invitation, after receiving expected letters from home, he might do so, if it could have the free, full and glad sanction of the church in the "Tabernacle."

The church at Christ Church, also sent him, the same day that the above offer was made, a telegram, inviting him to labor there, accompanied by a very substantial offer of support, indeed. This, also, for reasons somewhat similar, and somewhat dissimilar, to the above, Bro. Exley could not at present see his way to accept.

We have seen now goodly numbers of brethren at Auckland, Papakura, Wellington, Christ Church and Dunedin, and, taking all in all, the cause of a pure Christianity, apart from human imperfection, has made wonderful strides in these far-off colonies of the "home country," as the colonists seem affectionately, as well as proudly, to speak of the land of their birth. The brethren everywhere embrace a fair proportion of the intelligence and prosperity of their several

CHRISTIAN CHURCH, DUNEDIN, NEW ZEALAND.

communities, and in real piety will compare, all of
them, with the very best specimens in the States. In
some most vitally important matters connected with
the prosperity of the churches, and the happiness and
usefulness of preachers, the best churches in the
United States are at a long and a very halting pace
behind them. There is, we believe, no such thing as
a "subscription" list, as to how much this one owes
or that one will give. The brethren, being satisfied
with their choice of a preacher, offer him a really
substantial support, and pay it — pay it all, and pay
it at the stipulated time. Everything is done in
the solid English fashion, and we believe that the
churches, as a rule, will partake of this characteristic.
Now, would it not, in this age of Pan-Methodist,
Pan-Presbyterian, and other "Pan" gatherings, be
in order if the flag of a Pan-*Christian* Council should
be unfurled, and every mail-clad warrior of the good
cause, who may just now be tilting with lance, broken
or otherwise, with his brethren, concerning the organ,
open communion, or other real or supposed depart-
ures from the faith once delivered to the saints — if
each one would put his lance at rest on all these matters *just now*, and let there be a gathering of as many
as possible of the best and ablest, and most Christ-
loving, with the selection, and prayers, and benedic-
tions, and support of all the churches in the round
world, to consider — What is our mission? What are
our hindrances? What are the best means we can
employ to remove them? What are the best meas-

ures we can adopt to further the cause of an un-
adulterated gospel, and to win the churches to a
deeper piety, a more genuine union, and the various
religious bodies around us, to a calm and dispassion-
ate and earnest consideration of our attempted mission, and thus largely help to convert the world to
Christ? Great Britain, the United States, the Can-
adas, and these far-off colonies, as well as our thinly
scattered missions, could each furnish their quota of
good brethren, and all could be sustained for the time
being, from a common fund.

Once two ships-of-war met together in the darkness of the night, and in accordance with their real
nature, poured shot and shell into each other, until
the decks of both vessels were strewn with the fright-
ful wrecks of the dead and dying. When the morning light fell upon the scene, the Union Jack was
seen floating over each of the vessels! They *had
mistaken each other for enemies in the dark!*

When Nelson was once about to lead his line of
battle-ships into action, knowing that two of his
greatest commodores were at almost deadly enmity
with each other, he sent for Lords Rotherham and
Collingwood to come to his own flag-ship, and then
said to them, as he pointed in the direction of the
formidable French fleet, at Trafalgar: " Shake hands,
and be friends. *The enemy is yonder!* "

Is there not a possibility — aye, probability — that
brethren, and even churches, may be blundering, by
mistaking each other for enemies in the dark?

> Let His banner be unfurled,
> Banner of the Peaceful One;
> Wave it grandly o'er the world
> Till all strife shall be unknown.

Can we not differently try to make them into friends? Can we not find the enemy outside of our own ranks? God help us to do so; and then, with united front and united purpose, move on an unshaken host, to the help of the Lord against the mighty, and with the Almighty himself as our commander.

On some eight or more occasions, Bro. Exley preached to the church and congregation in the Tabernacle at Dunedin. The last Lord's day evening he preached, although it was an exceedingly wet night, the great building, which will seat about 800 persons, was well filled. The local press next day spoke of it as being crowded. He preached on " Beginning at Jerusalem," and, perhaps, hardly ever had preacher a more profoundly and apparently intensely interested audience. From first sentence to last, every soul seemed to listen as if fearful of losing a word.

Bro. Coop, on one Lord's day morning, as at Wellington and Auckland, gave a very earnest and tenderly affectionate address, urging the church to care with all its best solicitude for the children, and to cultivate the spirit of missions, and no small good would surely result.

We believe the general feeling in these colonies of

New Zealand is that of a thankful gladness for our
visit.

Bro. Coop left Dunedin for Melbourne, one week
before Bro. Exley, being anxious to receive any
letters waiting there for him from home. He had an
exceedingly rough and unpleasant voyage. On the
16th of December, Bro. Exley also left, embarking
on the Te Anau (all the vessels bear Maorie names,
Bro. Coop sailing in the Arawata), and had also an
exceedingly rough passage, with complete prostration
almost the whole time between the two ports.

South Pacific is a vast misnomer, as we found to
our cost. To pay tax to old Neptune under such
circumstances, was quite equal to making bricks without straw; and poor Christian in the dungeon of
Giant Despair, hardly suffered a more cruel usage
than we did. Still, now and then, some little incident crops up to spread wrinkles all over the face,
and create quite a diversion. On the last morning
before reaching Melbourne, Bro. Exley, having risen
early, to take a sea-bath, picked up a sixpence from
the floor of his state-room, in which were domiciled
two young men also, both of the novel-reading class.
Having ascertained that he had not himself lost it,
and to find out which of the two had, he quietly said,
" Have either of you lost anything? Have you lost
a sixpence with a small hole in it?" One of them
eagerly responded, " Yes, I have." " Well," said Bro.
Exley, " I have found a sixpence this morning on the
carpet, and it had *not* a small hole in it, at all." The

blank look which for a moment followed, and then
the bursting laughter, did a good deal towards recti-
fying the troubles of our poor and long-suffering and
rudely-tortured stomachs. *Apo-morphia* had, on this
six days' trip, fair play — and its influence was *nil.*

The cities of New Zealand really astonished us;
they are, indeed, marvelous affairs. We had the
notion that everything "go-ahead" was about an ex-
clusively American commodity. What a mistake!
Looking at the far-off state of these islands, and at
the naturally formidable difficulties in the exceedingly
hilly — even mountainous — condition of the sites
where each city has been built, it is doubtful to us if
anything more genuinely enterprising was ever done
in any State of the Union. Lofty hills have been
literally brought down, and valleys exalted, and
streets and roads laid out, and so wide and so well
macadamized, and side-paths so broad, clean and
substantial, and the streets so solid and level and
smooth, that the very best portions of the very best
American cities can not carry off the palm. The
buildings are wonderful in their taste and dimensions; the public libraries and reading-rooms, the
public museums and educational institutions, are not
surpassed by anything, if even equalled, in America.
The colonists are proud of their beautiful cities and
public institutions of all kinds, and they have abundant reason. Everything is solid. No such sign can
be found as, "Five dollars fine to drive over this
bridge faster than a walk!" There is an absence of

that "rush" which characterizes our American life,
and in its place there is visible a quieter expenditure
of the energies of life, and a wiser appropriation of
what belongs to the best of earth's joys — the joys
and comforts of "home, sweet home." All business
places of importance close early in the evening, and
the average hours of all classes of workmen are eight
hours per day. Loafers are neither found on street
corners nor lounging in stores, even in country places,
as with American little country towns; nor are business men ever seen lolling outside their stores, balancing themselves on half chairs. Business at present
is quite depressed, but improving. Gold is being
found in very remunerative quantities. Bro. T. Hislop, goldsmith, Dunedin, showed us a large mass, obtained by crushing the rocks in which it was found,
weighing, if we remember aright, more than 344
ounces. Farmers work only eight hours a day, like
the rest of the community, and they can afford to do
so better than the farmers of the West can afford to
be content with *ten* hours. Of many kinds of produce they easily raise two crops in the year.

Bro. P. Duncan assured us that on good soil it is
common to raise as much as sixty bushels of wheat to
the acre, and of oats in proportion. On inferior lands,
from twenty-two to twenty-six bushels of wheat, is a
fair average. And though the market — England —
is so much further off than for the Western farmer,
really, it is practically very much nearer, from the
fact that freights do not swallow half the value of the

crop, as in the West. The farmer seldom realizes less
than one dollar per bushel for his wheat, raises a
much larger quantity, at a less cost, and is every way
less burdened with heavy toil or severe alternations in
the weather, has but little hay to cut for his stock,
and but little more labor in winter to take care of it
than in summer. We were kindly taken by Bros.
Henderson, Lawrenson, Hislop and Battson, a drive
of some twelve miles, to see the Coöperative Woolen
Mills. It was a grand treat. Its gentlemanly man-
agers conducted us all over, and *better cloths* are not
made in the world. The best mutton is sold at the
meat markets at four cents a pound, and beef, the best
cuts, at six cents! The finest bread is ticketed up at
ten cents for the four pound loaf! Tweed cloths, not
to be excelled by the best makers in England, Scotland, or the States, are sold at about one and a half
dollars per yard.

Dunedin is about twenty years old, but its streets,
its stores, public buildings, churches, educational
buildings, are simply grand. We saw certainly one
little thing, but quite a set-off in its way, in a contrary direction. We were out visiting various places
of interest, when we stumbled upon, perhaps, the
smallest meeting-house we ever saw. Curiosity led
us to a closer inspection. It was about twenty feet
by eleven, and on the notice-board we read and
re-read the important information, "Strict Baptist!"
So "*strict*," indeed, that the whole thing was re-
stricted to about the above dimensions.

We wandered into the public Museum, free to the public, and were astonished to find many of the finest fossil specimens of the largest of the extinct races of creatures of both land and sea. Bro. T. Hislop has just erected in the Town Hall, itself both very extensive, and splendid in architecture, what is termed the largest clock in this hemisphere. He kindly ascended with us into the lofty clock tower, and showed us the machinery of this great time-keeper, and let us see, as well as hear, its beautiful chimes. It will bear his name to a very late posterity, should accident not befall the building.

It is difficult to describe Dunedin. Its business names are mainly Scotch and English. Its situation is beautiful beyond our power to describe it. Whether seen from the land side, or from the bay, it is a picture of loveliness. One of its local editors, so enamored with it, thus speaks of it, and he is an Irishman :

> A fairy, 'round whose brilliant throne
>   Great towering giants stand,
> As if impatient to obey
>   The dictates of her wand.
> Their helmets hidden in the clouds,
>   Their sandals in the spray;
> Go picture this, and then you have
>   Dunedin from the Bay.
>
> O never till this breast grows cold
>   Can I forget that hour,
> As standing on the vessel's deck,
>   I watched the golden shower

THE OCTAGON, DUNEDIN.

DUNEDIN, FROM THE N. E. VALLEY

Of yellow beams that darted
From the sinking king of day,
And bathéd in a mellow flood
Dunedin from the Bay.

Dunedin has three daily papers, issued morning
and evening, and three weekly papers — and all
edited with signal ability. We left it regretfully,
but very glad, indeed, that we had seen it, and especially that we had found so many there loyal to the
Saviour, and occupying so commanding a position.

Bro. Green, the preacher at the Tabernacle, was
formerly of Manchester, England, where he and Bro.
Coop were well known to each other.

We close this, promising but one more letter about
New Zealand, and then something of what we may
see in Australia.　　　　T. Coop, H. Exley.

LETTER VI.

WHEN we last wrote you of our whereabouts, we had just reached this far-off land of Australia; but before we say anything about Australia, it may prove interesting to many to add a few items more concerning New Zealand. Our deep conviction is, that as a country for those seeking new homes, it has advantages of a very superior character. The climate can not be equalled in any portion of the United States; while the prices obtained for many kinds of produce, so far, show that, though England as a market is much further off than the Western States of America, yet owing to the high rates of freight levied by the railway companies, practically the Western States are a long way further off from England than are these islands called New Zealand. There is an energy, a business capacity, an enterprise, which does everything in the most solid and enduring form, and, at the same time, such a determination that business cares and toils shall not usurp an undue overshadowing of the higher ends of life; that, perhaps, no business communities in the world have shorter hours of labor, take a larger number of holidays, or enjoy the brighter side of life better than they do here in

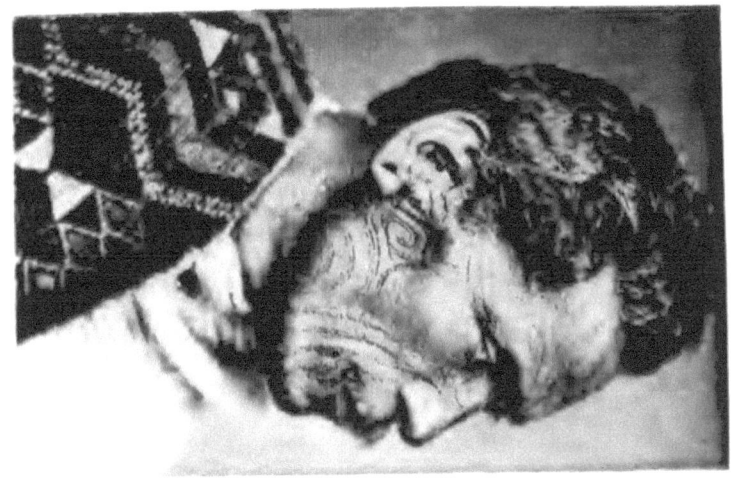

MAORIE CHIEF, TATTOOED.
New Zealand

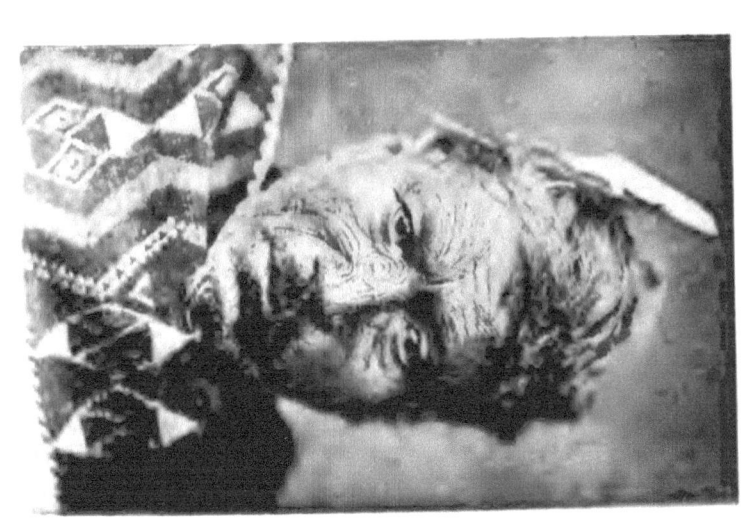

MAORIE CHIEF, TATTOOED.
New Zealand

New Zealand and the colonies generally. Their educational institutions, by-and-bye, will have no superiors in the world; and even now their common school buildings can not be surpassed for *extent, architectural finish* and *solid character*. There is nothing superior, even in America, to that which here is the *rule*. Their church buildings are not surpassed, nor even nearly approached, except in rare cases, in any of the cities known to us in America. The people are not simply religious, but *pious*, where religion is professed. England is reproduced all over the colonies, but with *improvements*. We have scarcely seen an American-looking face since reaching these far-off lands, and it may be that the influences of climate, soil, and general habits of life, will finally issue in a different type from either the American or the now everywhere prevailing English type. But the *character* will be always *English*.

Everywhere we heard the Maories spoken of as a very superior race indeed, and a universally expressed regret that they are so rapidly dwindling away. Their specimens of carving and house-building are evidence of great capacity, and those of them who have embraced the new order of things, and entered upon the path of Anglo-Saxon civilization, are reported to be exceedingly shrewd and capable as business men. In their savage condition, until recently, they were exceptionally cruel, all of them cannibals, and with a refinement of cruelty scarcely known to even the most ferocious of the red men of the West. Capt.

Cook did almost as much, if not more, than has been done by civilization, to extinguish cannibalism, by putting on all the islands a number of pigs. These so rapidly multiplied, that the Maorie found it easier and safer to hunt and spear a few pigs, than to go to war for the sake of feeding on human flesh. The descendants of those first put on the island by Capt. Cook are still found running wild. Bro. Caleb Wallis caught one of these some little time ago, and when subjected to more domestic conditions it became a very fine porker. The darkness, superstition and dreadful cruelty, which through unknown time have reigned in all these Southern lands, fill the mind with thoughts and feelings which perplex and confound. Perhaps one of the most baleful hindrances to the disenthrallment of the Maories from pure barbarism, is the superstition which rules over them. Large numbers of them are almost moved any way by one of their prophets named Te-Whiti. Quite lately he delivered to them a most remarkable speech, which, for a savage, is really a great effort. But if he had studied in the school of the darkest Calvinism, without any of its light, he could not have been more distinctly fatalistic. He strongly insisted that God from the beginning predestinated every thing to come to pass, that has ever, or ever will, come to pass; and to him they give heed. He told a large assembly of the Maories that, whilst through himself God had made it known that there was to be no more fighting between the Maories and the Colonists, yet neither

was there to be any mingling of the races, but that
each race must keep apart. A Colonist who was
present and heard his speech, and sought to reply to
Te-Whiti, was at once prevented, by Te-Whiti bidding the people to go home, when they at once dis-
persed. The most formidable obstacles in the way of
Maorie advancement lie in their social life. Their
communistic habits take away all stimulus to individual exertion and effort. Such of the *ponanga*, or
lower class, as work for Europeans, have no incentive
to save their earnings ; for if not spent upon themselves in meeting their own individual wants, they
are sure to be expended in one way or another on the
do-nothings of Maorie society. Occasionally one
more enterprising than the rest is found, who at-
tempts to acquire a little property for himself, but
finding himself "too heavily weighted," as one writer
very aptly terms it, drops back into the old state
again, a believer in *kai matatai* (food from the sea),
and the doles from the Native Land Courts. If one
should happen to accumulate property in the shape of
cattle, he is dragged down by those who only cultivate enough to keep them from starvation, having to
conform to Maorie customs, which is still regarded as
a paramount duty. Quite recently, at a potato planting, at a few hours' notice, in the very midst of the
season, all the able-bodied men left for a distant
settlement, to take part in proceedings consequent
on a witchcraft case. A few days afterward, a death
occurring at another settlement, the remaining part

of the population left to take part in Maorie customs over the dead; and thus the best part of the season was wasted. Things such as these are the real drawbacks to Maorie civilization. It is quite refreshing to hear all classes of the Colonists express a genuine regret that this fine race of people are so slowly emancipated from barbarism, and so rapidly dwindling away. There appears to be one serious mistake made by the Colonists in their efforts to civilize them, and it is this. The Maories present the peculiar spectacle, that whilst nearly all of them are able to read and write, and are eager to get knowledge, they yet have hardly any literature except religious. This can not result in the best outcome. Fanaticism is often the result amongst even white people who ignore all literature save that which is religious. It seems as if their prophet, Te-Whiti, was largely thus influenced, becoming more fanatical from the mixing up of old superstitions with ideas derived from the scriptures. Many of them are eager for knowledge, and one instance is related of a number subscribing together for the *Illustrated London News,* and though unable to speak English, have it read and translated to them by one who can. There is much hope for the young, but the old will pass away only half redeemed by civilization. We had it related to us, that when a body of Maories, some 800 in number, were undergoing their drill tactics, the quickest eye could not detect the slightest failure — all of them crouching as if sitting on a very low sup-

port, but in reality not sitting at all, and at the given
signal presenting the white palms of their hands first
in one direction and then in another, and this with
wonderful rapidity and unmarred precision, and then
suddenly presenting the full open palms of both
hands, first one way and then the other, but so suddenly that it had almost the appearance of a flash of
lightning. After this, and with the same astonishing
precision as if the whole 800 were but one man, they
leaped up straight and high into the air, and alighted
again on the ground, with such perfect exactness in
time, that the very ground vibrated for a long distance. When rowing their canoes, we were told that
the head is thrown back till it nearly touches the
spine, and forward till it falls on the breast, and with
a rapidity of action that is a wonder to Europeans.

When the Islands were discovered by Capt. Cook,
and until as late as but a few years ago, their cannibalism and cruelty were of the most dreadful character. Not many years ago, and near to Auhenega,
from whence we embarked when leaving Auckland,
as a party of Maories and one or two Englishmen
were pushing their way, six of the Maories went on
first, as scouts, being at war with some other tribe;
by and by a slave boy, belonging to the white men,
came running into camp, and saying that these six
had met with a woman, and had killed and eaten her!
Another party found a girl hidden under some mats,
when they dragged the poor girl out and killed her.
One of them cut off a leg, and took it at once to his

slaves to put in the oven and cook for him, using it
on the road as a walking-stick, holding the foot in
his hand. At the same time a man was fallen in with
by others, who was immediately killed and prepared
for the oven. Hearing this, the white men went to
the spot indicated, and found them cutting out the
bones of the dead man's knee. When asked why
they did that, they replied that the small bone (knee-
cap) would make a first-rate pipe-bowl, and the shin-
bone a flute! The hands they often fastened against
the walls of their houses, and the fingers so bent as
to hold fishing tackle or any other thing. In their
camp they had a white girl, with red hair. On the
white men's return from the scene just related, they
found the head of the girl in among the ferns; and at
the same time a Maorie came into camp carrying the
headless body of a woman on his back, with the arms
around his neck, and which he at once put into an
oven that happened to be preparing, and a slave,
using a wisp of straw, as the cooking proceeded,
rubbed off the dark skin, leaving underneath a flesh
as white as a European's.

Captives taken in war were often tortured, and for
this purpose were handed over to the women, who, in
war time, are said to have been the most cruel, and
subjected them to cruelties too horrible to relate.
Self-sacrificing missionaries labored hard and did
what they could; but one of the earliest of the white
men in New Zealand asks, of what use were the
blankets and Bibles of the missionaries, against the

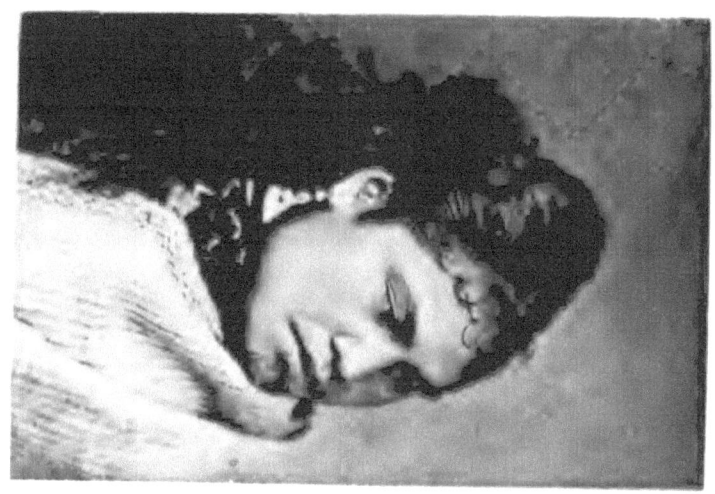

MAORIE WOMAN. MARRIED.

MAORIE WOMAN. NEW ZEALAND.

rum and muskets of the whalers and trading vessels?
Missionaries, from various causes, have found it, and
still find it, slow work amongst them. They believe
in a good and a bad spirit. When spoken to about the
soul, they would captiously ask the missionary how
he knew anything about it? When spoken to about
their false gods, they would get angry, and tell the
speaker to hold his tongue, or talk about something
else. They would often profess to believe what was
said; but it was in order to get some advantage over
the missionary, and afterwards indulge in merry
laughter at his expense. It is said that a Maorie boy
was sent to Howe, by the Catholic bishop, to be educated, and then sent back to New Zealand to be made
into a priest, but turned out so bad, he was expelled
from their school, and lived and diéd a bad Maorie.
The present Romish Bishop of Wellington, New Zealand, at a gathering of Catholics, in England, a few
months ago, stated that there were about 8,000 of
Maories in his diocese, and of these about 1,000, or
nearly so, were in the Roman Catholic Church.
Protestantism, he spoke of as the *leprosy* of Christianity. For these Catholic Maories, a church has
been built, and a catechism and other books printed,
at a cost of not less than $2,500 for each publication!
Catholic and Episcopalian efforts may seem, as far as
numbers are concerned, to succeed at least a *little*, but,
with whomsoever we talked, there was expressed a
doubt that indicated but little hope. Te-Whiti, one
of their chiefest prophets, has such a hold upon many

of them, that they put the most implicit faith in his
statements. Quite recently he told his followers that
very shortly the Son of Man will come, and restore
the Maorie to his place of rule and dominion on the
earth. An educated Maorie, the owner of a race-
horse, and living near Auckland, hearing this prophet
thus hold forth, and telling how the Lord would
come with the multitude of his angels, trample his
enemies under foot, and establish the reign of right-
ousness on earth, exclaimed with glowing eyes, "Is
not that grand!" Of a European standing by, he
asked, "Did you buy land on the plains?" On being answered in the negative, he said, "That is right,
for the Lord will come in his might, and by his own
power restore it all to the Maories." One night Te-
Whiti spoke for three hours, telling them that the
Lord was about to come, even that night. The night
passed, and the morning came, and still he did not
come; but the infatuated Maories believe in Te-Whiti
still. He takes care, however, amid all his prophe-
cies that the Lord is about to come and restore all the
lands back to the Maories, that he utters no words
that may invite to a breach of the peace. Perhaps,
hardly ever was there such a compound of ability,
heathen superstition and mutilated Christian knowledge, as meet together in Te-Whiti, and no influence
at work amongst this splendid race is more obstruc-
tive than his. Such crowds gather under his influence, that some epidemic, it is feared, will be the result; they live in such a limited space for the time

being, and under the worst kind of sanitary conditions. It may even become a necessity that steps be
taken to counteract the whole matter. The present
indications seem to be that the great body of adult
Maories will pass away civilized in some measure, but
wholly unchristianized. If the professed churches
were one, and these made united effort, there is no
just reason to doubt but the entire mass of them
would be speedily turned from darkness to light, and
from the power of Satan unto God. As it is, sectarianism operates as a crushing and blighting curse
— creeds are esteemed of more consequence than
souls, and sectarian shibboleths of more value than
the blood of redemption, shed for the salvation of
these benighted tribes of the children of men. Sectarianism, rather than see, at the expense of its creeds
and shibboleths, "a nation born in a day," would
look on, and with but a broken front seek to accomplish the impossible, and suffer the people to perish,
body and soul, unless they can be saved on the same
plan which suffers the people to perish at home.

We now leave New Zealand and its people, and in
our next will try to tell you something about what we
saw and heard and did in Australia.

T. Coop, H. Exley.

Melbourne, South Australia, Jan. 3, 1881.

LETTER VII.

WE ARE in Australia, the turned-up-side-down
part of the world; and we who *have not* done it,
have come hither also! What its *meaning* may be, is
still among the mysteries the future only can reveal.
If we were astonished at nearly everything we saw in
New Zealand, we are certainly not less astonished at
what we see here. As we pass over the "*Rip*," a
place " where two seas meet," for a vast space we see
the waters roll and tumble in great waves, and literally boil and swirl, and tumble over each other, as if
this was the great play-ground of the waves let loose
on a holiday. Passing across this exceedingly restless
" Rip," after a short time, passing over the Bay of
Port Philip, some forty miles in length, we enter the
mouth of the river *Yarra* (a native name, which
means flowing), and the magnificent city of Melbourne comes into sight — a city, with its suburbs, of
some 250,000 people, and which has grown up in the
time of many who came here strong young men, and
who are still but in the prime of life. The river is
crowded on either bank with vast industries of various kinds, and long lines of ships from the four
points of the compass crowd its wharves. As we
(76)

approached the city (our ship stopping at one point to
disembark the Government mails), a small vessel
drew near containing the oarsmen and one other
man; a young man passed down from the ship into it,
when we all knew that two long-separated brothers
had met. They flung their arms passionately around
each other, kissed each other, and patted each other
on the back, and renewed their embraces, till all eyes
were moist, and choking sensations felt in the throat.
The common human nature of all seemed to find
some measure of expression in the tearful joy of these
two brothers. By and by, as we drew near to the
place of landing, straining eyes were directed from
the ship to the shore, and from the shore to the ship,
in search of those since last meeting with whom long
years had intervened. A hat was seen to be lifted off
by one on the wharf, speedily recognized by one on
the ship, and in a few minutes Bro. Exley had grasped
the hand and given the speechless kiss, too overcome
to utter a word, to the only brother he had in the
world, Mr. George Exley, whose long separation had
lasted through twenty-eight years. Bro. Earl baptized him many years ago, and he is now one of the
deacons of the Lygon street church. Bro. Porter,
late evangelist of the Collingwood church, also came
to meet and give welcome to these Australian shores.
The voyage from Dunedin, New Zealand, to Melbourne, lasted six days, and was exceedingly stormy
and distressing. Bro. Coop having started a few days
before Bro. Exley, spent a little time at Hobart, Tas-

mania, and made a few very pleasant acquaintances.
The brethren there have just finished the erection of
a nice meeting-house, and are hoping to do a good
work for the Lord and Christ.

It is difficult to speak of Melbourne as a new city.
Taking it all in all, it has hardly a rival anywhere in
the world. We have both done some pretty *tall*
boasting in our time about America, but really we
just felt as if hit below the fair-fight line and had our
breath suddenly taken away. Melbourne, with its
magnificent streets and side-paths, its immense places
of business, its splendid public buildings, its large
number of exceedingly beautiful and large and solidly
substantial churches of all persuasions, its wonderful
Public Library and Museum, with its nearly 200
pieces of costly statuary, its galleries of oil-paintings
and water-color drawings, its immense Reading Hall
—itself one of the noblest and most imposing struc-
tures, magnificently appointed, with its lofty ceiling,
lighting, carving, gilding, its long rows of supporting
Corinthian columns, massive marble and granite—
and its Library of more than 101,000 volumes, with
immense globes, maps, etc., and every accommodation
for readers and students—compel unbounded admira-
tion, and a conviction that only a few of the oldest
and wealthiest cities of either old or new world can
at all compete with it. San Francisco, in many respects, is an inferior city in comparison. Surprise is
a feeble word to express our sensations—the more
we became acquainted with the city, the more were

we filled with a ceaseless delight. Perhaps no city in the world, certainly none of the same age, in either America or England, can boast of so many and such splendidly appointed and well kept city parks and reserves as Melbourne. The Zoölogical gardens are both very extensive; have one of the finest collections of wild animals — collected from all over the world — to be found, with few exceptions. Australia has a large number of wonderful serpents, and most of them appear to be poisonous to a deadly degree — quite a collection of them are to be seen in the gardens. The largest of all serpents we ever saw is here, and is of the Rock Snake tribe, and was brought from India. It is a terrible looking beast.

Adjoining the Zoölogical Gardens is an immense enclosure called the Royal Park. We do not know its dimensions, but it is very large. On New Year's day — here a beautiful summer day — thousands of the Sunday-school children were here enjoying themselves in all kinds of innocent games. A large number of immense tents were scattered over the park, and abundant provision was made for the wants of all. Our brethren were well represented — not less than three large tents were erected in different parts of the park, belonging to the churches of Lygon street, Collingwood and Hotham, and scholars, teachers and friends enjoyed themselves to the full. The town hall, for a new city, is an astonishing building, the like of which it would be hard to find in most cities. Its Public Hall — which seats 3,200 persons — has an

organ which they claim, for *power* and *quality*, to be
second only to the largest in the world.   It was built
by the same firm which built the great organ in the
Crystal Palace, Sydenham, London.   Its hight is 32
feet, and it contains more than 4,000 pipes, and cost
$35,000.   The hall commands $100 per night rental.
The post-office, considering the age of the city, will
bear favorable comparison with even New York city.
The government buildings, it is believed, exceed anything in America, except in a few of the oldest and
wealthiest States, whilst the streets have no superior
in the world.

Melbourne is the capital of the Colony of Victoria,
a region about 450 miles in length by 250 in breadth,
embracing only a few square miles less than Great
Britain, exclusive of the smaller islands.   Victoria
colony comprises about *one thirty-fourth part* of this
vast island continent.   It does not yet contain one
million of people; but of these ninety-five per cent.
are British subjects by birth, and only five per cent.
of foreign birth.   About 642,000 of the population
are Protestants, 211,000 Romanists, 5,000 Jews, 2,200
Pagans, and about 2,200 nondescript.   There are
about 119 males to 100 females in the population.
Nearly 1,100 post-offices, and a most efficient postal
service exists throughout the whole colony, and some
idea may be formed as to the business of the postal
departments, from the official report, that in 1879
more than 36,500,000 letters, newspapers and packets
passed through the various post-offices in the colony.

NEW LAW COURTS.

The colony has much more than 3,000 miles of telegraph line, and nearly 6,000 miles of wire in operation ; over which, in 1879, were transmitted 1,010,116
telegrams — one-fourth of which were on Government account. All the railways of Victoria are the
property of the State, nearly 1,200 miles of which are
open for traffic — about 4,000,000 miles were traveled
over in 1879 ; the total receipts from which were
nearly $7,500,000, leaving the Government nearly
$3,750,000 clear income above working expenses. In
1879 this little colony, and so thinly settled as yet,
had 210,105 horses, 290,436 milch cows, 894,436
other horned cattle, 9,379,276 sheep and 177,373 pigs.
From these facts it is a clear thing that Australia (for
all the other colonies are equally rich in these directions) will prove a very formidable competitor with
the great West, in the English markets. That competition has already successfully begun, and unless
railway freights are very largely reduced in all the
Western States, the West will have to beat a retreat.
Not only this, but the Australians are wide-awake
to the quality of their stock, and this is certainly of
a high order, compared to much of the scrub stock
which now finds its way to England from American
shippers.

Knowing that the *Standard* has a large circulation
among Western farmers, these items are given as being of real interest to them, so that they may take
steps to lose no market open to them, but so improve
as to keep and extend.

6

The Victorian gold-fields, since first discovered in 1851, have yielded about 49,000,000 ounces of gold, which, at twenty dollars per ounce, reaches the enormous sum of $980,000,000.

As an indication of the intellectual tastes of Victorians — the Public Library of Melbourne alone was visited by about 260,000 persons in 1878. Besides this institution, there are scattered through the colony 169 other libraries, athenæums, scientific, literary and mechanics' institutes, and possessing more than 221,600 volumes; and the buildings erected for them, in almost every instance, judging from what we saw, are not only substantial, but of great architectural beauty. These various institutions were visited during the year 1878, when no special excitement was urging them, by more than 2,600,000 persons. All these institutions, except one or two, are open to the public, free of charge. It is believed that the educational institutions and methods and results will compare favorably with those of any country in the world. It was officially stated by the government statist, that all the children in Victoria, between the ages of six and fifteen, were found receiving education during some part of the year, except about $7\frac{4}{5}$ per cent. Out of a population of less than a million by several scores of thousands, 227,037 children were attending school. Indeed, in whatever direction our inquiries extended, or our footsteps wandered, the conviction was forced upon us that the best informed Englishmen in England, who have not seen these colonies, are almost en-

tirely ignorant of what is being done here; and the
American who does not desire to modify his opinion
that America is ahead of all other countries in the
world, had certainly better stay at home.

Melbourne has no rival for a city of her years.
Victoria, like all the rest of the Australian colonies,
is some 10,000 miles further away from the great
centers of population, civilization and wealth of the
old world, than any of the States; and yet, with this
immense drawback, she can surely carry off the palm
in a large number of things, without which no city or
country can be truly prosperous. The entire State of
Iowa can not successfully compete with this one city
— Melbourne.

There is no such extreme poverty in this colony as
abounds in the large cities of England or America.
Melbourne, with her city-like suburban towns, contains about 280,000 people, yet we saw only sobriety,
cleanliness, and a universal neatness in dress.

The hours of labor are eight hours per day, beginning at 8 A. M., and closing at 5 P. M., with one hour
off for dinner. Saturdays, all quit work at 1 P. M.
Common laborers receive $1.80 per day, and skillful
workmen from $2.50 to $3.00 per day. Flour is
about three cents per pound, retail; mutton and beef,
about four to six cents. Clothing is cheaper than in
America, but dearer than in England. The people
take a large number of holidays — in which even the
most important public officers participate.

Christmas day and New Year's day both falling on

Saturday, we were surprised to find that even these
were all closed from Friday night in each week, until
the following Tuesday morning, except from 7 to 9:30
A. M. on Monday. Life here seems to be enjoyed,
and there is such a very marked absence of the rowdy
element, even on the most public occasions, that one
is compelled to admire the good order, self-respect
and law-abiding character which are marked traits of
the Australians, as far as our opportunities for forming an opinion enabled us to do so.

Under the guidance of Bro. J. A. Davis, we paid a
visit to the Exhibition grounds, buildings and exhibits; and here, also, the Australians may fairly
challenge any city on earth that is of the same age as
Melbourne. The buildings are not simply of an extent required by their international character, but
grand in conception and execution. They stand in
the midst of an immense public square, containing
nearly a hundred acres, laid out as if with fairy wand
directed by a poet's eye. The fountains, statuary,
shrubbery, trees and flowers, are all laid out with the
most exquisite skill and perfect taste ; the whole of
the grounds enclosed by an iron fence both lofty and
very beautiful, the like of which we do n't recollect
seeing anywhere but surrounding some of the great
parks in London. As we went through the various
departments, it was very evident that in all classes of
Australian exhibits, especially in silver and gold,
woolen fabrics and machinery, in their several departments, Australia is abreast with the foremost, and

need not fear any. The machinery would be a credit
to the best firms in the world, and it is clear that if
Australia should import much, it would be because
her demands are larger than her present facilities can
supply, and not because of any deficiency in skill.

We had a very pleasant interview with Rev. Mr.
Rantoul, Presbyterian minister, formerly of Southport, England, and also with Rev. Mr. Chapman,
Baptist minister. He told us the Baptists numbered
about 2,000 members in Melbourne. They are open
communion, and *very* open. Their church edifice is a
splendid affair, and their school-rooms are of a fine
order. You may be sure that we were busy enough,
in one way or another. Bro. Coop gave addresses to
the brethren of Lygon street, Collingwood, Unity
Hall, Hawthorne, and one or two other places, on
missions and Sunday-school work ; whilst Bro. Exley
had hardly touched Melbourne, although wearied out,
almost, with six days' tossing on the sea, before he
was pressed into the service. The meetings were
such that, so far as known to us, we have no such
meetings in England or America, save in few in-
stances. Bro. Exley preached on " The Beginning
at Jerusalem," in the vast Music Academy, to an audience — although it was one of those almost intoler-
ably hot days which now and then sweep over the
land — of more than 1,500 people. On more favorable evenings, Bro. Haley has an audience of more
than 2,000! We have no meeting-houses, so far as
known to us, west of the Mississippi, at all to be com-

pared with those in the colonies, for capacity, solidity and school accommodations. Davenport, Iowa, and Dubuque, come nearest. The membership of the various churches of the brethren in the city and the suburbs, is about 1,400 to 1,500. Bro. Haley is the Evangelist in Lygon street, and now that the services in the Music Academy are closed for the season, the church in Lygon street is crowded. Last Lord's day evening, after the address, quite a number, some eight or ten, went forward. Bro. Bates, late of Christ Church, New Zealand, is the evangelist of the church in Collingwood; Bro. Yates, of North Fitzroy; Bro. P. Brown, of Footscray, and Bro. Colburne, of Hotham. Besides these, there are churches of considerable strength and ability, meeting in Unity Hall, Swanston street, and Prahran, the latter of which has a good, substantial church, but which is now unsuitable, and they are about to build a larger. All of them have Sunday-schools where they have facilities for them, and good ones, with efficient staffs of teachers and officers. There is also another church at Hawthorne, only feeble as yet, besides several churches scattered at distances of from four to thirty miles from Melbourne. Bro. Haley was right when he said, "We know how to set preachers at work, who come around these parts." We had ample proof of their ability in this line. Bro. Coop spoke in nearly every one of the city and suburban churches. Whilst Bro. Exley preached some sixteen times amongst them, although never strong any of the time.

One thing is very noticeable in all the colonial churches — they sing. All seem to esteem it a precious part of the worship to sing, and they sing as if they felt it was a *privilege.* Bro. Exley insists that, whilst personally loving the organ, and having no objection to it in worship under some circumstances, yet that to introduce an organ here would be an impertinence, as well as an intrusion, and out of place, if used to lead or improve the music where such singing is maintained as we have heard; and that the shortest way to settle the music question is to get the heart so filled with praise that the lips must utter it forth; and at once to stop all controversy about the organ. But some fear (troubled consciences especially) that Bro. Exley's idea is a dangerous one — and it certainly is, if the wonderful words are true, lately spoken in the Edinburgh Free Presbytery, by Rev. Mr. Balfour and Rev. Dr. Begg, that "hymns never came alone. Their introduction invariably opened the door for other innovations in the direction, for example, of instrumental music and artistic singing"! Was there ever human wisdom, so much of it, crushed into one sentence before? If these gentlemen are right, then Bro. Exley is wrong, and we had better let the *hymns* alone; also, lest their use should bring in artistic singing, and so corrupt the simplicity of Christian praise, let us have recourse to "*guid* hard *psaums,*" read or sung in *in*-artistic manner. We spent Christmas day at Bro. Alfred Shaw's hospitable home, whose beautiful house and grounds, instead of looking, as they

are, but a few years old, wear all the appearance of a
genuine old English home, with the best taste and art
employed to lay off the grounds and make every
thing look beautiful. Here we saw oranges or lemons,
we forget which, perhaps both, the trees bearing
*blossoms, fruit just forming, well grown fruit unripe,
fully grown fruit, and ripe,* all on the same tree! Bro.
and Sister Haley, Bro. George Exley, and Brethren
Coop and H. Exley, put in a great day there, Bro.
and Sister Shaw showing us every courtesy. The
day was finished off by a large balloon being sent up,
to find if it could, and give welcome to, the incoming
New Year, 1881, and bid a kindly farewell to the old
one, 1880. Bro. J. A. Davis, a gentleman whom
Bro. J. B. Rotherham baptized in England many
years ago, with his excellent lady, made us most welcome to their hospitable mansion, also inviting us to
make it our home during our stay in Melbourne.
They invited quite a nice company of Brothers and
Sisters to a social cup of tea, to meet us and spend a
pleasant social evening together. From all we know
and can learn, the cause has taken deep hold in Melbourne and surrounding suburbs and country in the
colony of Victoria. The *material* composing the
churches is such as we feel sure would gladden the
hearts of the brethren, both in the United States and
all over Great Britain. Their path has not been a
smooth one, nor is it likely to be; but the brethren
have done a grand work, and are awake to the necessity of putting forth all their strength to maintain it

and extend it. Sister Haley is doing a good work in teaching a large singing-class, in connection with the church on Lygon street. Bro. and Sister George Greenwell have both safely arrived from England, and are looking well. Their destination is Adelaide, in the Colony of South Australia. He will, it is hoped, be of real service to the churches. There is work here to do which he is well qualified to do, and which, perhaps, he has been brought here providentially to do.

On the 8th of January, Bro. Coop, leaving Melbourne for Adelaide, left Bro. Exley to follow a few days later, so that he could preach at Collingwood the next Lord's day, in the absence of Bro. Bates.

At this point we drop our mutual pen, and promise, the Lord permitting, to resume it again in the city of Adelaide; only further saying that, so far as we know, our visit has not been in vain, and that all would be glad to see us again.

T. COOP, H. EXLEY.

MELBOURNE, Australia, Jan. 9.

LETTER VIII.

LEAVING Melbourne, Jan. 10th, 1881, after some fifty hours' sailing, we reached in safety the city of Adelaide, the capital of South Australia. Bro. Hindle, late Evangelist in England, and who is now occupying the pulpit of the Grote Street Church, until the return of Bro. Gore from America, together with Bro. Smith, Evangelist of the church at Hindmarsh, Adelaide, and a daughter of Bro. George Greenwell, of England also, were all on the wharf to give us welcome, as we stepped on shore, saying, " Welcome to South Australia! "

The voyage was very stormy. Indeed, it is to us an evident mistake to call these waters, the South *Pacific.* Since sighting the shores of New Zealand till now, every time we have been on the sea we could most truthfully sing,

" Storm after storm rises dark o'er my way."

However, we reached in safety the city of Adelaide, " *The Beautiful.*" Whilst Melbourne is the capital city of the colony of Victoria, Adelaide is the capital city of the Province and colony of South Australia. Besides these large regions, there are

three other immense tracts of country, each one large
enough to become the seat of great nations, viz.: New
South Wales, Queensland and Western Australia.
The region called South Australia, and which is all
comprised within this one colony, has an area of 914,-
930 square miles, or about 585,427,200 acres, and
stretches across the whole island-continent, from the
Southern Ocean to the Indian Ocean.

The colony was founded in 1836, and many of its
first settlers are still living to see the fruits of their
daring, courage and enterprise. Standing on a spot
of ground facing to the sea, at Glenelg, some six
miles from Adelaide, and under a very large natural
arch formed by the bending over of a very large
Blue Gum tree, until three of its limbs touch the
ground, at a distance of about forty feet from the
trunk, stood Sir John Hindmarsh, R. N., on the 28th
of January, 1836, and proclaimed this country a
colony of the British Crown. January 28th is the
National red-letter day of the South Australians. At
this time, Port Adelaide, about eight miles away, had
not been discovered. By the kind courtesy of Bro.
T. Magarey, whose sea-side residence is close at hand,
we were taken to see it, and stood under the venerable
arch, perhaps on the very spot from whence Sir John
Hindmarsh had proclaimed the colony, some forty-
four years ago, and distant about one mile from the
spot where the first Pilgrim Fathers landed. Since
then, there has been witnessed the successful experi-
ment of planting a free colony on a free soil, where

liberty flourishes without licentiousness, and where,
also, the daring, restless and expansive energy of the
present, has not — nor seems likely to — broken away
from the traditions of the past. It seems to be certainly true, that here, the freest of free political and
religious institutions flourish harmoniously side by
side with a profound regard for and attachment to the
monarchical institutions of the mother country, of
which we never heard them speak but with the realest
affection — and always speaking of England as *Home*.
They boast of possessing the broadest form of political and religious liberty, and along with that a very
marked absence of lawless excess. They are a grand
proof that religion can flourish without a State
church, and they possess a government — one by
themselves, and for themselves; and that without
losing their attachment to the institutions and government of the land that has become the fruitful
mother of such mighty nations.

This one colony of South Australia is in length
about 2,000 miles, by about five hundred miles in
breadth — a very vast region, truly. It has a population, however, of only some 260,000 people, at the
utmost. Of these, about 5,000 are aborigines, but
they are rapidly dwindling away. A bare recital of
what may look like common-place facts, and without
the slightest desire to boast, may certainly give a
large and very legitimate pride to every South Australian.

The colony was founded on principles directly op-

posed to a State Church, and yet two-thirds of the
entire population have provided themselves with
places of worship. Over 900 churches and other
buildings have been erected for worship, containing
about 150,000 sittings. About eighty-five per cent.
of the population are Protestants, and the other
fifteen per cent. Romanists. The Church of England
has the largest membership, but the Wesleyan Methodists have the larger number of places of worship.
There appears also to be a most active and efficient
Sunday-school work carried on, as about 40,000 children attend the Sunday-schools, or one in six and
a half of the whole population.

The institutions for the relief of the sick — hospi-
tals for the poor, outcast, blind, insane, old and
infirm, deaf and dumb, and for even inebriates — are
so many and so well provided for, that it is believed
that this little handful of people does more to bless
humanity and to put something of divine sweetness
into the cup of human bitterness and sorrow, than
did the whole Roman Empire during the whole thousand years of its existence, from first to last.

As an indication of the thrift of the Colony, it may
be observed that there was exported in 1879 to the
value of $94.80 per head for the whole population,
whilst the imports reached the same sum, and a small
fraction over. Among the exports there were 90,000
tons of flour and 442,000 quarters of wheat. There
is no question but what the great Western States will
have formidable competitors in breadstuffs in all

these colonies, as well as in beef. In 1879 fully seven
and a half millions of dollars in breadstuffs was exported from this little Colony alone. Besides this,
they exported some 56,000,000 pounds of wool, and
of splendid quality. Nearly two-thirds of the export
trade of this Colony is absorbed by Great Britain.
There has just been completed and perfected an Australian Reaping Machine, which, by a very simple arrangement, also threshes out the wheat in the cleanest
manner. We were told that it was not ready in time
to be entered in the list of Australian exhibits in the
International Exhibition now being held in Melbourne. It is, however, pronounced a success. South
Australia already exports to England reaping ma-
chines. Indeed, there are a large number of articles
produced or manufactured in these Colonies which
will prove no small competitors against all other
countries in the English markets.

The total liabilities of the eight South Australian
banks are but little more than one-half of their assets.
The bank buildings are marvels of architecture, both
for splendor and extent.

In 1879, this one Colony, containing but a com-
parative handful of people, possessed 133,000 horses,
266,000 horned cattle, 6,000,000 sheep, 90,500 pigs,
and 11,200 goats. Since their copper mines were
first discovered, but a few years ago, they have exported more than $80,000,000 worth of copper. They
have built more than 620 miles of railway, and are
rapidly extending their old lines and building new

ones. They have built more than 3,300 miles of
highways, very broad, and of such a solid character
that it is very doubtful if the entire West from the
Missouri could show in the aggregate, not only so
many miles of *decent* roads, but outside of cities anything comparable to these. Nearly 1,000 miles of
these roads are built in the most thoroughly solid
manner, and metalled to the depth of some eight to
ten inches with the best material. We have not seen
even a small country bridge but what is so substantial
that the heaviest trains and weights could be run over
it *ad libitum*. The larger bridges are very fine and
strong, built to last for generations. One of them,
stretching across the river Murray, is 1,900 ft. long.
Besides all this, these enterprising colonists have
actually built more than 4,400 miles of telegraph
line, and of this nearly 2,000 miles form one continuous line stretching from Adelaide in the south to
Port Darwin in the north, thus stretching across the
entire continent, and over 1,350 miles of the country
entirely unsettled by white men. Iron posts are used
over the larger part of the line, and both posts and
wire had to be carted over the whole distance. Wells
had to be sunk at many points for water; a serious
number of the horses died, and one-third of the bul-
locks, but in spite of all difficulties, in less than two
years this great trans-continental telegraph line was
completed, bringing South Australia into telegraphic
communication with nearly the whole civilized world,
and done and paid for by a population of, then, less

than 900,000 souls. The natives often attacked them
as they made their way across this almost *terra incog-
nita*, but after they had received a few shocks from
the batteries, they let the wires alone, and spread consternation among their savage friends, calling the
telegraph the *"white fellows' devil."*

The city of Adelaide, with its suburbs, has a population of some 40,000 people. It is one and one-third
miles square, with five large reserves of park grounds,
so located as to be both exceedingly ornamental and
conducive to the health and beauty of the city, and
also laid out and planted with trees, shrubs and
flowers, and well fenced in. The streets are all laid
out at right angles, and are equal to anything at least
in this half of the world. The entire city is surrounded by a belt of park lands nearly half a mile
wide, reserved by act of Parliament for the health,
pleasure and recreation of the people. Every evening, except Lord's day evening, when fine, the game
of cricket is played by large numbers of people.
Bro. D. Galle, a gentleman connected with the press,
and well known in Adelaide, as he drove us around
the city, assured us that he had counted, on a Saturday afternoon, as many as forty games of cricket
being played at the same time on these park-lands,
and not big boys merely, but by the strong muscle,
bone and sinew of the city.

Two daily papers, of eight large pages, are published in the city, each of which also appears in an
evening edition. Their morning editions are about

View in the Botanic Gardens.—The Rosary

10,000, the evening not so large. Each office also issues a weekly. One of them, as large as the *Standard*, contains forty pages, filled with the best reading, and forming a continuous history of the colony. The other issues also its weekly, in large and handsome form, and contains twenty-eight pages. Besides these, there are some thirty other papers published in the Colony, and several religious periodicals in addition. Indeed, their reading-rooms, museums and educational institutions indicate a people very forward to understand and secure the advantages of a wide and liberal culture. Common school education is compulsory between the ages of seven and thirteen. The text-books are on a graduated scale, approved by the Government; and no teacher, highest or lowest, is allowed at his own sweet will, as but too often happens in the Western States, to the great detriment of the pupils, to change them, and substitute others. The salaries of the teachers, paid out of public funds, vary from $500 to $1,500. In the city of Adelaide there is a University being erected, standing on a reserve of five acres, which Government has endowed with 50,000 acres of land, and five per cent. in addition on all sums donated to the Institution. Already two of its wealthy citizens have each donated the sum of $100,000. No religious tests will be required of either professors or students.

The city of Adelaide is especially rich in churches. Indeed, it has so many, that whilst Melbourne, because of its large number of grand public buildings

7

now being erected, is called "the city of unfinished
palaces," Adelaide is called the "city of churches."
Its churches are so many, and so large and beautiful,
that it is evident that the people are, on the whole,
both well-to-do and pious.

Through the kindness of the Hon. Philip Santo,
member of the Legislative Council (Upper Chamber),
Bro. Exley had an introduction to the Hon. Thomas
King, Minister of Public Education, from whom
he received a splendid volume on the History of
South Australia, just issued from the press, and with
inside pockets and maps, and gotten up in the best
style of the publisher's art. The honorable gentleman was exceedingly kind, and seemed glad to have
the opportunity to put into the hand of a stranger
seeking information anything belonging to his department. Under his administration, educational matters are not likely to flag.

With Bro. D. Galle as cicerone, we visited public
institutions of all kinds, and in all the utmost courtesy was shown. Going into the Government Land
Office, the walls hung 'round with maps of all sec-
tions of country open to settlement — large maps
attached to endless canvas bands, passing over rollers
— we had the entire system of land conveyancing ex-
plained by the chief of the department. The beauty
and size of the public buildings, such as the post-
office, town hall, law courts, banks, museums, schools,
etc., is such that to describe them would almost subject one to the charge of "Australian blowing." We

have traveled a good deal, and seen a good deal, but
have not, we venture to say, considering the years
and the circumstances, seen anything at all to be compared to Melbourne and Adelaide. Were we Australians, we *would* " *blow,*" and not be ashamed of it;
but as we are only a stray Englishman and an Anglo-
American, we will only say that, whether Great
Britain thinks she has reason to be proud of her
stalwart daughters or not, the daughters have abundant reason to be proud of themselves.

The Botanic gardens of Adelaide, under the superintendence of Dr. R. Schomburgk, a gentleman who
is a member of nearly all the learned societies of
Great Britain and Continental Europe, are almost
indescribable for their order, extent and beauty. In
these respects, they astonish even those who have seen
Central Park, New York, and the Kew Gardens,
London. The plants in these gardens, exclusive of
florists' flowers, are nearly 9,000; whilst the trees are
not only many and very various, but so arranged as
to make the spot one of the loveliest in the world.
Here there is everything to delight the eye and
gratify the most cultivated taste. The oleanders, for
size, mass, color and fragrance, exceed all we ever
saw, either in England, Jersey, or elsewhere. It is,
however, a very curious fact that the beautiful china-
aster, so universally — and deservedly so — a favorite
all over the West, here is only a small and insignifi-
cant flower. And the chrysanthemum-aster here goes
back to its original type.

The gardens have one of the finest of palm-houses,
and filled with the rarest plants; they have also a
splendid museum, ferneries, and houses for all kinds
of tropical growths. They have also a large aviary,
for the purpose of acclimatizing foreign birds. Of
course they have acclimatized the English Sparrow,
but, like the Americans, they seem to have been
victimized by the introduction of the *House* Sparrow,
instead of the *Hedge* Sparrow, and consequently the
fruit is no small sufferer from its depredations. The
gardens also contain a very respectable collection. of
wild animals, gathered from nearly all points of the
compass—many of them, however, peculiar to Australia.

On the plains, and in addition to all the ordinary kinds of fruit common to England and the
United States, there are grown, and in great perfection, many others, such as figs, lemons, oranges, nec-
tarines, almonds, olives and citrons.

Before leaving Adelaide, Bro. Thomas Magarey
favored us with a ride around the city, and then took
us out to his country estate, some eight miles away, to
Enfield House. For a private gentleman, he owns
one of the largest telescopes we have seen, outside
of public institutions, and one of great range and
power; and to keep it fitting company, a very large
library also, and stocked with some of the choicest
books. With him, religion is not a matter of form
only; he is, in all the best senses of the words, a
godly man. He seems to be more a man of deeds

than many words. He holds views on John iii. 5, perhaps in full accord with what is called Plymouth Brethrenism, but by no means discarding the connection between baptism and remission of sins. More, perhaps, we ought not to say, beyond this: that his views concerning the work of the Holy Spirit, and the believer's possession of it, whether incorrect or not, are very far removed from that soul-benumbing theory, that there is nothing but the *Word alone*.

We were conducted all over his well-arranged home, fitted up with extensive bath-rooms, for every kind of bath, except salt water, that being some miles distant. From the top of his house, a vast expanse of land and sea is visible. His gardens have in them olive, lemon, orange, with a large variety of other trees, amongst them the *kharob*, or locust tree (*ceratonia siliqua*), from which we obtained a few pods, such as the Prodigal would fain have eaten to still the cravings of his hunger. Bro. Magarey assured us that the olive would yet prove to be of great commercial importance. Our visit, with its kind courtesies, will not soon be forgotten. T. COOP, H. EXLEY.

ADELAIDE, South Australia, Jan. 15, 1881.

LETTER IX.

As INTIMATED in our last, this country, South Australia, is destined to be a great oil producing country, and olives are planted out on a liberal scale. The oil is a better article than any imported. Sometimes, however, fierce hot winds from the north (all hot winds here are from the *north*), sweep over the country, exceedingly trying, but not so prostrating as some of our hot days in Nebraska, when the fruit of all kinds, on the side exposed to them, is literally "*baked*." The rain-fall in Adelaide is only nineteen to twenty-one inches, but in the Mount Lofty Range, but eight miles off, the rain fall is 40.677. The mean temperature of an Adelaide winter, is 54° to 55°. The winter months are June, July and August. The spring months of September, October and November, are said to be the most genial months in the year, the average temperature being about 60° to 70°. The general average production of wheat in the whole region cultivated thus far in South Australia, is about nine bushels and forty-eight pounds per acre, and this for the past twenty years. The cost of production is, however, small, and the quality is such that it commands the highest price in the English market. On

the side of health, South Australia, so far as present
statistics show, will compare favorably with any country in Europe. From a very able pamphlet issued
by our brother, Dr. Magarey, it is evident that,
whilst for infants under twelve months old the death-
rate is a shade heavier than in the most favored
European country, the death-rate for adults is much
less; so that, as Dr. Magarey says, "the Colony af-
fords a good chance of them living to a good old age."

There are about eighteen tribes of natives living in
this part of the Colony, none of them numerous, most
of them dwindling rapidly away. Some of them
used to have a special propensity for stealing *fat people* from the other tribes and eating them! If a man
had a fat wife, he was very careful never to leave her
unprotected, lest she should be siezed by prowling
cannibals. Their history is involved in great ob-
scurity. The first boat which they saw filled them
with terror. The first oxen which they saw — two
stray ones from a far-off ranche — they thought were
demons, and fled from them in the wildest fear, calling them by the expressive name, *wundawityeri* —
that is, beings with spears on their heads — and ever
since they have called all cattle *wundawityeri* — a fine
illustration of the manner in which new names get
coined. They are very expert in throwing the
"boomerang" and "*kaike,*" or reed-spear. The reed-
spear is a long, slender, tough rod, with a point of
hard, heavy wood, about a foot long. They throw it
with a *taratye,* or throwing-stick, and with such force

and precision that it has been known to kill a man at
nearly 300 feet, and passing through a tough bark
shield also. The natives attribute all diseases to
witchcraft, and their methods of cure are absurd
enough. The doctor will sometimes kneel upon the
sick man, and squeeze him until he groans out in
agony — a method very much like that of some muscular M. D.'s among even white men, who pound and
knead their victims in order to cure them. Often-
times a gray-bearded old father will execute a solemn
dance before his sick son, beating time to a kind of
cymbal, called a *tartengk*, and utterly divested of all
clothing, and feel that he has done wonders towards
the recovery of the patient.

Missions have been measurably successful. Still it
is to be feared that in some parts of this vast island
continent the method employed to make them Christians has been that recommended by an old shepherd.
Two natives having been arrested for killing another
of their tribe, the old Scotchman suggested that they
should be hanged; but who, when doubts as to the
justice of such a course, in view of their manners and
customs, were expressed, said: " I dinna think that
we ought to care much aboot their manners and customs at a'. We ought to mak' them gie up a' sich
hathenish practices. Sure, it's our dooty to do a' we
can to mak' Christians o' them. Hang them, by a'
means, sir; I say, hang them! Sure, it's our dooty
to mak' Christians o' them!"

The first time that some of them gathered into the

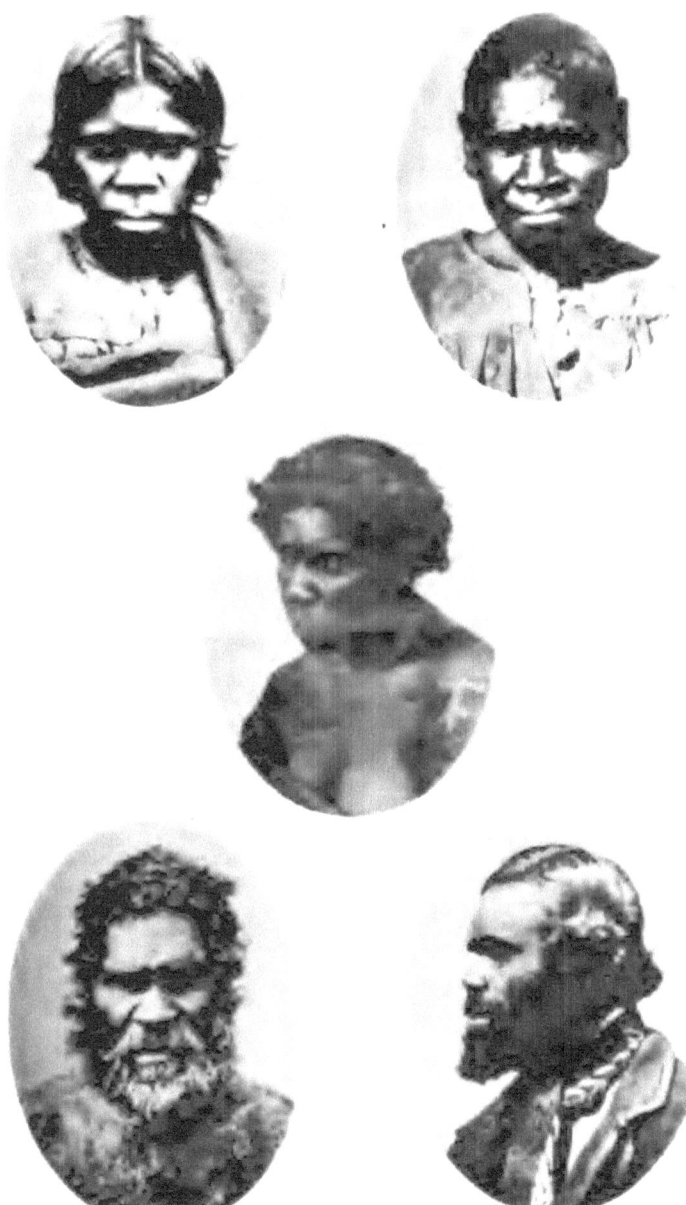

Missionary's house, when they heard the clock strike, they listened in astonishment and fear, and then whispered, " What him say?" and then rushed in fear out of the house. Infanticide was very prevalent among them, until the missionary gave the mothers rations of flour, tea and sugar, until the little ones were twelve months old, and the practice at once came to an end; but before that the babies were put to death as soon as born, and sometimes with horrible cruelty. We saw a few natives; some of them are really good-looking; they are very straight, and walk with all the dignity belonging to savage nature, and receiving favors from the whites, receive them as from equals. Many of their customs are of a very barbarous character, with many curious rites connected with them, and involving much suffering, but of their origin or meaning they can give no account. It is very reasonably supposed that these customs, in much better form at one time, had a meaning which is now lost, and are only observed from superstitious motives, and that the natives have descended from a higher state of civil.-zation. The weapons which they possess are also of a kind which it is said they could not invent in their present state. The " boomerang" and throwing-stick are both of this kind. The " boomerang," when first heard of, suggested a new idea to even scientific men. They are said to have no power of invention, and the power of calculation only in a small degree. They can imitate what they see others do, but it seems impossible for them to originate anything fresh, or even to improve on the methods they have been taught. Everything about them indicates that man, in a state of barbarism, so far from raising himself into a state of civilization, inevitably and always goes down towards extinction. The intelligent among the South Australians speak of a time when their people were more numerous than now, and that their numbers had been decreasing long before the advent of the white man amongst them. The first comers possessed so much of civilization that they were enabled to increase in numbers; but as soon as they became corrupt, they had then reached a point where their barbarism rapidly tended to their extinction. Savage life is fatal to the increase of the human family. It is, indeed, most strikingly true of all the savage tribes of the Colonies, as of the red men of the West, "If ye live after the flesh, ye shall die." Their decrease is rapidly hastened since the introduction of the vices of the white man. It does not seem at all likely that if man had been created in a condition as low, or lower than that of these aborigines, that he ever could have arisen out of it. What is very remarkable about them, is this: their language, though very limited, possessing not more than about 4,000 words, is yet a very highly organized language, and remarkable for its complexity of structure, the number of its inflections, and the precision with which it can be used. Those who have studied it, look upon it, not as a language in

process of formation, but as rather the remnant of a
noble tongue, now becoming extinct. It has six
cases in each declension of nouns and pronouns, and
a double set of pronouns for the sake of euphony and
expression. Verbs are regularly formed from roots
consisting of one vowel and two consonants, or two
vowels and three consonants. They possess the
faculty of readily learning other languages, but have
no power to invent language. Their pronouns have
three numbers, the singular, dual and plural. Not
only have they all the *cases* we have, but several
others in addition. The dual number, in some of the
declensions of nouns, has *eight* cases, and all regularly
formed. Surely, a barbarous people is utterly un-
equal to all this, by any process of evolution yet discovered. There is a very curious and very striking
similarity between many native words and some English or other words, both in sound and sense, as, for
instance: the words Dlomari, the *gloaming;* Marti, for
mortar; Limgari, the *tongue;* Napi, *nupta*—a spouse;
Ngo, *go.* There is no evidence whatever, notwithstanding the character of their language, to indicate
that of themselves they could advance from barbarism to civilization. Some facts would seem to indicate that even white men going among them, but
without any set purpose to either seek to elevate
them or to take care of their own higher culture,
would be far more likely to become barbarized themselves than influential for the elevation of the natives. Bro. T. Magarey told us of a white man who,

having strayed into the bush, and supposed to be lost,
after some fifteen years turned up again. He had
been living amongst the natives, and was almost as
black as themselves, and, whilst able to understand
English when he heard it, found it difficult to speak
it. One day, as a herdsman was tending his cattle,
he saw this man, coming timidly and stealthily along,
and at once called to his assistant to bring him
the gun. The poor fellow understood that, and lifting up his hands, stammered out, in the best English
he could command, "Do n't shoot! me British *obs-
jeck.*"

During our stay in Adelaide, we were domiciled
at the beautiful home of the Hon. Philip Santo.
Every kindness was shown to us, and the best of care
taken of us. Bro. Coop addressed the churches of
Adelaide, Hindmarsh and Norwood, on Sunday-school
work and missions. Bro. Exley addressed the same
churches on other themes, and to audiences it was a
joy to look upon. Bro. Santo is one of the elders of
the church in Grote street. During our stay here,
the brethren held a grand tea-meeting in Grote street
church, to give us welcome, and brethren from a
distance came to participate in it. Letters, also,
from some who could not be present, were read, giving us welcome. Bro. and Sister George Greenwell
were both present, and he gave us one of the most
touchingly beautiful addresses to which we ever listened. Of course we were called upon to contri-
bute our share of the talking, and Bro. Exley fin-

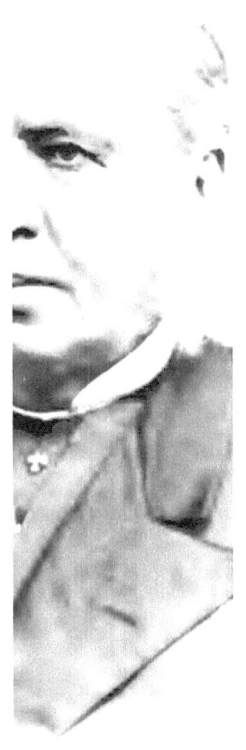

PHILIP SANTO.

ished his speech by singing them his favorite song —

> "Oh! the good we all may do,
> While the days are passing by."

The churches in all the colonies seem to be very partial to tea-meetings, and a most enjoyable affair they make them. We have attended three of them. The church in Grote street, Adelaide, numbers about 450 members, and all living in peace; the church in Hindmarsh about 300, and the church in Norwood about seventy. These last two are both in the suburbs close by. Besides, there is still a fourth in Adelaide, of about sixty members, if we remember rightly, in which Dr. Vercoe is a very earnest and active member, a gentleman whose medical reputation stands very high, and once a member of the church at Chelsea, London.

Then there is still a fifth church, with a very respectable meeting-house, presided over by Bro. Hussey, a gentleman baptized many years ago by Bro. Campbell. He is an earnest believer in, and as earnest a pleader for, the doctrine of the near approach of the Second Advent of the Lord from heaven. There is a constant interchange of preachers, I believe, amongst them all. The churches all have large Sunday-schools, except the last one. That at Hindmarsh numbers about 300, with a Bible-class of young men of about thirty members, and another of young women of about the same number. Connected with this church, they have a large and, we

think, the best arranged Sunday-school hall we have
seen. The great hall of the Sunday-school will seat
between 300 and 400, and has *nine* class-rooms besides, five down one side, and four on the other side
of the hall. Bro. Smith is the evangelist, and Dr.
Kidner, well known to many in England, one of the
elders. There are several other churches in the
colonies, and some of them have good, substantial
church buildings.   .

The population of the colony does not exceed 260,-
000, yet our brethren are one to every one hundred
and seventy-five.

Adelaide, with its suburbs, has a population of
about 40,000. Our brethren number amongst them
about 900, or one to every 44, nearly. In London
our membership is probably not more than one in
every 10,000; in New York, about one in every
5,000; in Birmingham, perhaps one in every 1,200,
and in Cincinnati, about one in every 400. Some of
these are only conjectures, but the disparity between
the membership in the colonies, and the best of
the churches in either England or America, in not
small.

For the most part, while faithful to the traditions
of the apostles, they are not heresy hunters, and have
but little sympathy with Procrustean methods. Our
intercourse with them, will, we trust, prove fruitful
of good. It has been very pleasant, and whilst the
claims of homes, so far away, render our departure
necessary, we shall leave with regret.

On the 22nd of January, Bro. Coop will sail for England in the " Garonne," of the Orient Line, leaving Bro. Exley to labor here a little while longer.

T. Coop, H. Exley.

ADELAIDE, South Australia, Jan. 20, 1881.

LETTER X.

OUR LAST letter was posted to you just before Bro. Coop went on board the *Garonne*, of the splendid Orient Line of steamships. Bro. Santo, myself, and a few others, went down to the Semaphore to see him embark. We saw him safely on board, and then our little steamer turned away, and, owing to the proximity of another ship, we lost sight of him almost in a moment — Bro. Coop entering upon his long voyage, and myself to return to Adelaide, to labor for two Lord's days more, and then to embark for Melbourne, and thence to my far distant home, probably by way of Suez, Turin and London.

Since the injury sustained in San Francisco, the journey through Palestine became more and more an undertaking it did not seem prudent to enter upon; and so on this account, together with other important matters, with unspeakable reluctance I gave it up. Well, notwithstanding that, my face is "steadily set towards" the New Jerusalem and the painless, sorrowless land ; and so I joyfully sing —

> Yonder 's my house and portion fair;
> My treasure and my heart are there,
> And my abiding home.

(112)

Returning to Adelaide, I spent two more Lord's days there, and preached about five more discourses.

On Monday, January 31, in company with Bro. Santo, I left Adelaide, embarking on board the Claude Hamilton, for Melbourne, and a more comfortless voyage could hardly have been. The decks were literally impassable, from their being covered with the company and material of Cole's American Circus.

I spent four more Lord's days in Melbourne, preaching in some seven different places. The number of churches in Melbourne and suburbs, all of which are really a part of this great city, is a splendid testimony to the energy and untiring perseverance and self-sacrifice of our brethren here. If there is anything to be compared with it in either Great Britain or the United States, I have never heard of it. I will endeavor to give a few items, which I trust will be of real interest to all churches, and help to stimulate them to love and good works.

There are some seven churches in the city and *immediate* outskirts, besides many others at short distances. Five of the seven churches in the city occupy their own church buildings, which are about $36,000 in value, and possess a seating capacity for about 3,000 people. They all have flourishing Sunday-schools, with over a thousand scholars, and a proportionate number of teachers. Four of the churches employ an evangelist each, all the time — Brethren Haley, Bates, Colburne and Yates.

8

The church meeting lately in the Unity Hall, have rented the large and very handsome church edifice called the John Knox Church, formerly occupied by the Presbyterians. This church, considered by some to be too narrow, is one from which *broader* churches may learn divine lessons in many directions. It is the *mother* of all the rest, if I am rightly advised. It has no evangelist at present, but is seeking to obtain one. It paid about $15.00 per week towards the expenses of the Sunday evening services in the Music Academy. It sustained an evangelist at Footscray. Its care for its poor and sick, I believe, has no parallel amongst the brethren, so far as known to me. It is very strict on the communion question, has no organ, and in church worship has the open platform, but under the presidency of men of sound wisdom and judgment; and it is foremost in assisting the good work in other places. It is a church with a large heart and an open hand. The Lord grant it a very great future. Bro. Haley preached at the opening of the new premises, and had a fine audience. Every church in all the colonies, no matter whether it has an evangelist or not, meets every Lord's day to break bread. This is universal, without a single exception.

Before leaving Melbourne, accompanied by Bro. Santo, quite a number of us rode out to a little country village called Broad Meadows, where we have a little church of faithful, earnest and pious disciples. Out of their very moderate means, they have just completed a very nice little place of worship. Our

visit was a real treat to them and to us. The social
tea-meeting was a success, and the after-meeting, with
Bro. Santo in the chair, gave joy and gladness to all,
and will not be very soon forgotten. The country
around Broad Meadows is like a bit of Nebraska —
only not so good. The public houses, on the high-
way-side in the country, are so many as to compel
observation. Nothing but a very large and constantly moving population can give them more than
a very moderate support.

Before leaving Melbourne, I was again called upon
to preach for Bro. Haley, and selected for my subject, "The Final Resurrection." After showing the
possibility, probability, certainty, agency and extent,
in order to impress upon the minds of all how easy it
is for Him who is the Resurrection and the Life, to
bring out of these earthly, natural bodies, bodies
incorruptible, immortal and *spiritual*, I made use of
an imaginary handful of common garden soil as a *natural* body, and then, after apparently holding it up
and crumbling it to dust, held up a magnificent
bunch of flowers, furnished me by Bro. and Sister
Davies. I spoke of that as but the *spiritual* body,
brought forth from the formless dust, and asked,
How had the Great Architect built up *that?* How
had the Great Artist painted *that?* How had the
Great Chemist perfumed *that?* And emphasized the
thought that He who could transform the dust of the
ground by the kiss of the sun — and the mysterious
forces of earth and air — into such unspeakable

beauty, could be at no loss in the Great Day of
Resurrection, to bring forth from these already beautiful natural bodies of ours, bodies glorious, powerful, immortal, incorruptible and *spiritual*. The impression made will last all through this life. This
was my last discourse in Melbourne, save that I lec-
tured once, on Milton, Cromwell and their times.

On Tuesday, March 1, I embarked on board the
Maugana, for Hobart, being persuaded by the brethren to visit the church there for six weeks, in connection with the opening of a new church building. For
once, the sea trip of some twenty-four hours, from
Melbourne to entering the river Tamar, Tasmania,
was enjoyable, the sea being calm and smooth. We
have land in sight most of the time as we cross Bass'
Strait. Little is seen save birds and porpoises, and
now and then an albatross with wide-spread wings,
ten feet from tip to tip, balancing itself as it swiftly
skims over the restless waters — sailing away in the
distance, or circling 'round about, as if in sport, then
returning to the ship, and passing it with the swiftness
of an arrow, albeit we are going from ten to twelve
miles an hour! Gannets, or the Solan goose, are
seen riding fearlessly on the waters. They are about
the size of a common goose, but with a much greater
stretch of wing. Besides, almost countless numbers
of mutton-birds are seen skimming the sea in the distance. The flight of these birds, or some other,
which go in vast numbers, and so near to the surface
of the water, has more than once led to the convic-

tion that the beholder was really looking upon the movements of the sea-serpent.

Entering the river Tamar, a splendid stream, we have a river journey of forty miles through very fine scenery, until we reach the city of Launceston. In Tasmania, the counties, cities and rivers, are nearly all named after places and rivers in England. It is a matter for never-ceasing wonder how, in these far-off regions, all the cities, without exception, have put up such a large number of such large, solid and beautiful public buildings of all kinds, as are to be seen in these colonies. Here there are the counties of Dorset and Devon, a Cornwall, Dorchester, Exeter, Ilfracombe and Launceston, at the head of the Tamar. The Great Colony of Victoria and the city of Melbourne were founded by explorers from Launceston in 1835. Launceston has some 10,-000 inhabitants, and for these it has erected thirteen large, solid and handsome churches. It has also a fine Town Hall, with organ to match. All the streets and side-paths are good. Among its public buildings and institutions it boasts a *Workman's Club*. It provides not only a well-stocked library and a table well supplied with papers, but amusements also. It is managed entirely by the artisans themselves. It has a lecture-hall, piano, reading-room — a billiard-room, bagatelle-room, and others also. Chess and draughts are favorite games, as also skittles. Smoking is allowed everywhere, except in the rooms devoted to the library and reading.

It is nearly eighty years since Tasmania was num·
bered among the British Colonies, but it does not yet
count more than about 120,000 inhabitants. Hobart
is the capital city, with about 25,000 people. It
is built on the river Derwent, and for beauty of situation may fairly challenge at least all the colonies put
together. It is surrounded with magnificent mountains, the principal of which is Mt. Wellington, about
4,200 feet above the sea. The purple mist which
covers ˙ it like a beautiful veil, is a never-ceasing
delight to look upon. Bro. Carr, who is remem-
bered, and esteemed and loved for his work's sake
here, and Bro. Gore, with others, have had the rich
pleasure of toiling to its summit, from which, I am
told, one of the most glorious of visions of mountain,
valley, city and sea, is to be seen. I am not equal to
the ascent, and so feast my love of the grand and
beautiful, by looking to the hights to which I can not
ascend. The climate of Tasmania is one of the finest
in the world, and the death-rate, at least amongst
children, is less than almost anywhere else in the
world. The river is filled with vessels of all sorts,
and quite an amount of business is done here in *Tin*,
which is found and worked in large quantities; and
also in the precious metals. Farm interests are not
in the most flouishing condition here. The population of the colony is only as stated above, not more
than 120,000. Yet they possess nearly 2,000,000
sheep; of cattle, 130,000 head, and 25,000 horses, and
about 40,000 pigs. The quantity of wool exported

in 1879–'80, was 8,333,726 pounds — value, $2,250,-
000. In 1879, there was gold found to the amount
of $1,200,000. The amount of tin found is at the
rate of $1,000,000 per year. Splendid fruits of many
kinds are exported in large quantities, for so small a
population, and all the small grains, which are of
very fine quality.

Education is compulsory, at ages ranging from
seven to fourteen years, and is unsectarian in character, and large encouragement is given to the higher
education of all who care to possess it, by a system of
exhibitions at the best private schools, and by annual
examinations for the degree of Associate of Arts,
under the direction of the Council of Education.
Two scholarships, of a thousand dollars each, tenable
for four years at a British University, are awarded
annually by the Council of Associates of Arts, on
passing a prescribed examination. The land, however,
seems to be hampered by unwise restrictions, and from
which, at present, we in the Far West are free. There
is, without fair question, however, a great future
before Tasmania, and all these Australian colonies.

One of the saddest of all the facts connected
with this Island of Tasmania, is the complete extinction of the native tribes — *not one being now
alive!* William Lannae, the last man, and Truganini, the last woman, are both dead. In this letter,
however, I can say nothing concerning the native
races, but promise another as soon as I can find the
time to write, which probably will not be until I can

once more embark for the home that seems such a
long way off. I will fill up the remainder of my
space by a short account of my visit to this city of
Hobart, where I am at the present writing. Arriving here on the 2nd of March last, in the evening, I
was met by Bros. Smith and White, and conducted to
very comfortable apartments.

The brethren here are about 120, all of the hard-
working class, with a few of the business community
amongst them. The energy, self-sacrifice and abound-
ing faith of these brethren, if imitated by all our
brethren, would carry victory at all points. They
have just completed a very substantial brick church,
with stone facings, plain, but very neat, and capable
of seating 400 persons. It fell to my lot to open this
church building for Christian worship on Lord's day,
the 6th of March. The audiences were large, and
apparently deeply interested. On Tuesday following,
we had a public Tea Meeting, at which more than
300 persons sat down; the place was beautifully fes-
tooned with ivy, ferns and flowers, with a large number of flowering plants tastefully arranged on stands,
and which were kindly furnished by various friends.
The Tea, singing by the choir of young brethren and
sisters, with the various addresses, made a most enjoyable evening. The brethren here are close communion, *but not heresy hunters.* They preach the
gospel, using the talent they have in the church, have
had but little evangelistic help, have the mutual
teaching, doing the best they can, and even though

they have been a long time without evangelistic help,
they have never omitted to break bread in the morning, or preach the gospel in the evening as best they
could. They have had no small burden of difficulties to bear from various causes, but they have strug-
gled on to something like a position from which they
may move on to victory. It is almost the only church
of our brethren in the Island, and no finer field could
the American Board of Missions select than this. In
about one year the cause in Hobart would be self-
supporting — that is, if the preacher were reasonable
in his requirements, and this he would be sure to be,
if a *true* missionary spirit filled his heart.

At the opening of our first evening meeting, a
most untoward event took place, throwing a heavy
gloom over the church. Scarcely had the first hymn
been announced, when a large, fleshy lady fell suddenly sick, and by the time she was lifted out of the meeting-house, into the porch, she was dead. On the
second Lord's day, at nearly the close of the evening
service, another lady was carried out in a dangerous
condition, but she fortunately rallied again in a short
time. These two events filled us all with a good degree of fear.

During the five weeks I have labored here — and I
came not knowing even one person in the church or
city — it has been my unspeakable gladness to lead
down into the waters of baptism eleven persons, and
a spirit of inquiry has been awakened in others. Bro.
Moysey, kindly given up by the church at Chelten-

ham, Victoria, is here to succeed me. He has come
for three months, so that the work may have some one
to carry it on. Bro. Moysey is an able man, and is
much beloved and esteemed here for his work's sake.
The church at Cheltenham not only gives up Bro.
Moysey to come here, but, with rare self-sacrifice and
loving devotion to the Lord Jesus, *also pays him just
the same as if he were still laboring* for them, the
churches of Melbourne finding from its local brethren supplies to fill his place. Here is a grand way in
which in many places amongst us at home, real missionary work can be done. May some such work be
largely done for his name. I came here a stranger,
but that mysterious power which is in the gospel, has
made me feel so much at home, has linked me to so
many brethren and sisters, that whilst home tugs hard
at the heart, it is hard to leave, and I feel a heavy
sorrow. Since coming here, I have been the kindly
and even tenderly cared-for guest of Bro. and Sister
Bradley and their gentle daughter.' Of all such, in
view of their work of faith and labor of love, it may
be most truly said, that "they are redeemed unto
God." I have worked, since coming here, almost
without intermission, but believe that I leave here,
physically, a stronger man.

I have no space to tell of the beauties of the *Fern
Tree Bower*, some five miles distant from Hobart, and
situated at the foot of the monarch Mount Wellington. Through the kind courtesy of Bro. Speakman,
I was taken by his daughters (the youngest of whom,

Miss Sarah Speakman, I have baptized) to see it.
Strange indeed are the growths of these far-away
lands; and a few leaves of the Fern Tree I bring
away with me as mementoes of my delightful visit.

The river *Derwent* is really an arm of the sea, and
can afford ample anchorage-room for half the fleets of
the world. A trip in the little steamer to Kangaroo
Point, and a stroll on the beach, listening to " what
the waves are saying," is wonderfully refreshing, after
weeks of almost ceaseless toil.

At Hobart, also, as in nearly every city we have
seen, there are splendid public gardens, and perfectly
free to the public; also a very extensive Public
Library, in which the visitor has nothing to do but
take down from the shelves any volume he desires, sit
and read at his leisure, and replace it himself, or leave
it for the Librarian to replace. If there is any volume desired which the visitor can not find, the courteous Librarian will at once get it for him. Alongside
the library-rooms there is also a large reading-room,
and the best papers and quarterlies and monthlies in
the world lie on the tables. Reading-rooms and
Library are always well attended by both ladies and
gentlemen. In addition to these there is also a large
Parliamentary Library, of some 8,000 volumes of
choicest selection. This also is *free.* Into this I
often went, hunting up items of interest concerning
the now extinct native races. Hobart also has a very
fine Museum. I think I can safely say that in these
directions, in this out-of-the-way corner of the world,

larger privileges were within my reach during the six weeks of my visit, than ever fell within my reach in twenty years' residence in the West.

On Saturday morning, at 8 o'clock, April 16th, I bade adieu to Hobart, and waving good-bye to friends known only for a short time, but not to be forgotten again, our train moved off, and in six hours I was once more in Launceston. Embarking on board the *Mangana*, on Lord's day morning, at 8 o'clock, after an exceedingly stormy and distressing voyage of twenty-four hours, I am once more safely in Melbourne, but too late to obtain a berth on the *Orient*, which sails to-morrow for London. Visiting Bro. Haley, I had the pleasure of seeing for the first time Bro. Gore, who has just arrived from America, and is looking quite well. Through the courtesy of Mr. Posisti, the member for Richmond in the Victorian Parliament, I was shown all over the houses of Parliament and the very extensive library connected with them, and then conducted to the roof of the buildings, from which one of the most extensive views of the city and far distant country is obtained. The buildings themselves are so extensive and so magnificent, that to describe them is utterly beyond my power. Arriving in Melbourne too late to secure a berth, I have consented to go, at the urgent desire and request of Bro. Haley, up to Sydney, New South Wales, to help the brethren there for two months, before embarking for home; that is, if the brethren there desire my help when I get there. They have urgently solicited Bro. Haley to send them some one, and so I am about to go and visit this other great colony. Concerning New South Wales and the churches, I will write (*D. v.*) in due season.

A letter has just reached Bro. Haley from Bro. Coop, posted at Cairo. He was quite well, and, from what he says, had a most interesting time on the voyage, preaching several times and organizing a debating society, the subject for debate being, " The Colonies of Australia, or the United States of America — which are the most desirable fields for those who are seeking for new homes?" Of all this you will hear in due time, perhaps even before you receive this.

I will only further say in this letter that, the Lord willing, I shall stay not longer than eight weeks in Sydney, and then embark for home, going around by way of Suez, London and New York, and, if prospered on the journey, reach home about the middle of August, resting a day or two at Davenport, Long Grove, and West Liberty, Iowa, on the road.

HENRY EXLEY.

MELBOURNE, Australia, April 13, 1881.

LETTER XI.

LEAVING Tasmania before I could find time to write out a few items concerning the native races, I now shall try to do so. One of my first questions, after seating myself in the cars, when going to Hobart, was about the native Tasmanians, and my surprise was great indeed, when told that the last one of the entire race, Truganini, a woman, was dead, having died but some five years ago.

When the island was discovered, in 1642, Nov. 24th, by Abel Jans Tasman, the natives, whilst never very numerous, yet numbered, it is supposed, about 7,000, of all the tribes together. As I stood by the bedside of an old settler, near eighty years of age, and one who had been in the country more than fifty years, I asked him to tell me how the natives were treated by the white men; and as he slowly shook his dying head, he very mournfully said, "Very bad; oh, very bad!" Whilst it is fresh in my thoughts, let me say that this old man, whom it fell to my lot to consign to the grave, and one of the most trustful and triumphant of Christians, seems to me a far more wonderful case of long abstinence than that of Dr. Tanner. For eight weeks before his death he rarely took any sustenance whatever; but for the *last thirty days* of his life he was known to take but two spoonfuls of rice, two spoonfuls of beef tea, and twice the yolk of an egg in a little wine, and which his stomach rejected. A little water and wine was all he took for at least twenty-eight days, and for fully thirty days prior to that he rarely took anything. There is no doubt about this, as I questioned closely the two or three friends who were his nurses. His great age and long abstinence seem to me a marvel by the side of which Dr. Tanner's fast does not look an unreasonable thing, or at all to be questioned as to its being honestly carried out.

David Collins, Esq., for a long time the Judge Advocate of New South Wales, was the first Governor of this beautiful island of Tasmania. He was present with his father at the battle of Bunker Hill, and there witnessed that event which was accepted by all Europe as the sign that the American colonies were lost to the British Crown. He proclaimed the dominion of Great Britain over this island, and thus announced the first day of a second and rapidly growing great empire, in the place of the one he had witnessed as lost. He married an American lady, and died in 1810.

Society in Tasmania in that early time was not very choice. In 1802–3, there were at one point 400 male prisoners (for then it was a penal settlement), and but twelve free settlers, three married women, six unmarried, six children, and forty marines. Out of such a condition of things as this, a large amount of the cruel slaughter of the natives seems to have certainly grown. The morality of the time may be estimated in a measure from the following: The first wedding published by the *Tasmanian Press*, reads thus: "On Monday, the 26th ult., R. C. Burrows to Elizabeth Tucker, both late of Norfolk Island. They had cohabited together for fourteen years, thus verifying the old adage, 'better late than never.'" The very excellent highway from Launceston to Hobart, 130 miles in length, was constructed by convicts. Thirty-three years ago there were not less than 28,459 convicts on the island. One of these, a man of gigantic stature, ran off, intending somehow to go to China. This man, whose name was Buckley, with another, wandered for months in the mountains, suffering great misery, where he found a tribe of natives, and lived with them thirty-three years, conforming to all their barbarous customs. When found, he had forgotten his own language, was dressed in a kangaroo skin, and armed with spears. Another proof of the degradation of a white man, coming into close relations with the savage, when that white man is himself but partially educated, and at the same time utterly surrounded with barbarism. His own measure of civilization seems to have been completely swallowed up in their barbarism, except that he helped to give to his countrymen, at a later date, a friendly reception amongst the natives. He was still living in 1852.

The first settlement was made in 1803, and by such

a class of persons, almost all convicts, that it is only
too readily conceivable how the poor native would
fare at the hands of the white savages escaping from
convict discipline. Sitting in the Parliamentary Library, and reading of the doings of some of these,
it made me feel as if to smite these miscreants with
the fiercest lightnings would be but small retaliation.
In the words of Prescott, when speaking of Las
Casas' "Short Account of the Destruction of the
Indians:" "It is a tale of woe. Every line of the
work may be said to be written in blood." Mr. Mel-
ville, in his work on Van Dieman's Land, says:
"Were it possible to record and detail the murders
committed upon these poor, harmless creatures, it
would make the reader's blood run cold at the bare
recital."

Mr. Backhouse, another writer, and a benevolent
gentleman, living at that time, says of the outrages
practiced upon them, "That they were such as to remove any wonder at the determination of these injured people to drive from their land a race of men
among whom were persons guilty of such deeds."

Dr. Dixon, the Episcopalian Bishop of Tasmania,
says: "There are many such on record, which make
us blush for humanity when we read them, and forbid
us to wonder that the maddened savages' indiscrim-
inate fury should not only have refused to recognize
the distinction between friend and foe, but have
taught him to regard each white man as an intruding
enemy."

9

Count Strezdeck, in his work on missions, p. 360, says, what may be applied with equal truth to Tasmania as well as to the Dutch at Cape Colony : " The Christianity which was offered the natives was stripped of its charity, and the civilization embraced no recognition of his rights or property. They therefore rejected both."

So far as I have been able to make out, and I searched in the Parliamentary Library a good deal, the whole race of Tasmanians seem to have been completely blotted out of existence, with scarcely any trace of Christianity attaching to them.

One of the most remarkable of facts connected with the black race of Tasmania, is this: that though the native women had been and were most cruelly ill-treated by the whites, the male aborigines, though ready to inflict death by the spear, always abstained from violating the person of the white woman. The author of " The Last of the Tasmanians" says: " In all the incursions made by the blacks into the settlements, it has never been known that one white woman has been violated by them. The nearest approach to that crime has been done by half-civilized natives, who invariably became the greatest ruffians in the war. Not until they had become more degraded than they originally were, by learning the vices of the whites, could they be guilty of the atrocities which they afterwards committed."

An old convict servant of the author just named, said to his master: " They fought well. I admire

their pluck. They knew they were the weaker, but
they felt also that they were the injured, and they
sought revenge against many odds. They were brave
fellows, and I would have done the same." Scenes
have been witnessed on this Island of Tasmania and
deeds done very much like those which the Dutch en-
acted in the early settlements of New York and Long
Island, when the Indians rose up to revenge the cruel
treachery and slaughter inflicted on them, and carried
a fierce war into every Dutch settlement in the region.
When Captian Cook saw the natives of Tasmania in
1777, they were quite naked, wore no ornaments, they
were quite black, and not disagreeable looking; had
beautiful teeth, good eyes, but were very dirty. They
were of full average hight, very sinewy and wiry, and
when fire-arms were first shown them, they manifested neither curiosity nor fear. No canoes were
ever seen among them. They bore a certain resemblance to the negro, whilst the Australian had
often the appearance of a European. They were
somewhat shorter in stature than the European, but
when young, heavier in proportion to age. One girl
at eleven years of age weighed 102 lbs., and another,
at eight years old, eighty-six lbs. The average of
European children, as compared with these, is as
sixty to eighty-six, and seventy-eight to 102. When
first discovered they showed but little of that ferocity
and vindictiveness which afterwards so characterized
them. They were rather timid and distrustful at
first, with a marked indifference and lack of curi-

osity.   All ideas as to their origin and destiny seem
to have been erased from their minds.   But it appears that their language is indicative of considerable
strength, copiousness and mental power and activity.
Their social relations were characterized by the absence rather of what is venerable and lovely, than by
the presence of what is dark and revolting.   Polygamy, to some extent, seems to have prevailed among
them (but some doubt this), and the condition of the
women was abject enough.

From all that can be gathered now, it seems quite
clear that when the whites first settled in Tasmania,
the natives were mild, diffident, willing to be friendly,
and rather afraid of the invaders of their territory.
But when the *convicts* who had served their time began to be let loose, and others escaped from confine-
ment, and those who had *"tickets of leave"* began to
steal the wives and daughters, and to kill the husbands and fathers, then they became ferocious, and
attacked the settlers wherever they found them.   If
cunning and something approaching to treachery had
not been employed against them, many of them
would have been found living in their forest homes
to-day.   *They were slaughtered, often that room might
be made for the sheep and cattle!*   Then the few that
remained were forcibly deported (like the red men of
the West have often been) to an Island in Bass
Strait, where, scantily supplied with what, to them,
were necessaries of life, they lingered awhile, and,
pining for their homes on the mainland, which was

just visible across the Strait on a clear day, they died.
Others of them were subjected to as cruel, wanton,
and merciless slaughter as ever were any of the
Indians of the West. Sitting and reading these
things in the Parliamentary Library, the *natural* man
flames out, and the cry almost escapes, calling for
vengeance on the wrong-doers.

The Tasmanian had but little affection for his wife,
and in the hour of parturition she was left alone with
another woman, and in a few hours had to follow her
tribe as best she could, with her child hung on her
back in a Kangaroo skin. If the child required
nourishment, the *breast* was thrust up to the shoulder
to the child, and this custom accounts for the fact that
the breasts became disproportionately long. If the
child was permitted to live, it was treated with great
care, but very often the children were destroyed; but
this barbarous custom was not common with them,
when first discovered, but the *result of continual suffering inflicted by the whites!* The young men were
initiated into the state of manhood, by being severely
cut with some sharp instrument on the breasts, shoulders and thighs, and this was done by an aged female;
but though the flesh was made to turn back like a
crimped fish, they were in the highest glee during the
whole operation. They had no dogs until they were
introduced by the whites, when they kept numbers of
them around their encampments, the pups being often
suckled by the women! When the men were absent
on a hunting expedition, the women would sing a

song addressed to a deity who presided over the day,
for protection for their husbands and themselves, and
to bring them back in safety, and accompanying with
gracefulness of action the song which they poured
forth in strains by no means inharmonious. Mr.
Davies, in the Tasmanian *Journal of Science*, said
that " the sweetness of their notes, and which were
delivered in pretty just cadences and excellent time,
made a harmony to which the most refined ear might
listen with pleasure." They turned away from fat
with loathing and nausea. A party being removed
to Flinder's Island, the captain had some soup made
for them. They looked upon it quietly, and then
skimmed off the fat, and put it on their hair, thinking
it was made for that purpose, but they would not
drink the soup. They even rejected bread with dis-
gust, if it had been cut with a butter-knife. They
seem to have left behind them no trace of their oc-
cupancy of the Island, beyond the large heaps of
shells on the beaches, the remains of their feasts.
These shell-mounds have been thus made, and not, as
has been too often supposed, by the change in the
relative positions of the land and sea. Heaps of
shells, and mounds several feet in thickness and many
yards in breadth, abound along all the shores, and on
every indentation on all the coast, but always thus
produced. They had stone implements, and obtained
fire by rubbing two pieces of wood briskly together,
but have no tradition as to how they obtained the
knowledge. They are said by high authority to be

nearer in likeness *to the whites*, and not to the worst amongst them, than the so-called cïvilized peoples of the cities would be willing to admit.

The cause of the animosity which at last could not be extinguished except by the extermination of the blacks, seems to have been this: A small stone house had been built for a gardener, who had just begun his work in cultivating around it, when one day, as he was working, he was surprised by the appearance of a number of natives coming toward him; at which he ran off and told Lieut. Moore, who commanded a party of the 102nd regiment, stationed there. He at once drew up his men to resist the expected attack. On the approach of the natives, the soldiers were ordered to fire upon them. The execution this volley did among them, and their ignorance of the nature of firearms, terrified them to such a degree that they fled without attempting the slightest defense. From that moment a deep-rooted hatred of the strangers possessed them, which seems never to have been put down. *Moore was drunk.*

The Hobart Town *Gazette* of 1824, says of them: " The sable natives are the most peaceable creatures in the world." I read such stories of cruelty and enormous wickedness, as made me almost wish that the whole white race had been exterminated.

Dr. Ross says that, in 1823, when he went to one point, he saw a man sitting on a stump, nearly starved to death. He had only three days before stolen a black woman, and chained her to a log with a bullock-

chain, dressing her in a fine linen shirt, the only one
he had. This he had done in hopes of taming her.
She somehow contrived to slip the chain, and escaped.
Not long after he was found speared to death. Another case illustrative of the almost incredible wickedness of some of these early settlers is told by the
author of the "Last of the Tasmanians," as follows:
Two men went out shooting birds, when a number of
natives, happening to see them, fled away. A woman,
very far advanced in pregnancy, being unable to run
with the rest, climbed up a tree (and they were
very expert at climbing). She broke down branches
around her for concealment, but she had been observed by the sportsmen. One of these proposed to
shoot her, but the other objected. The first one,
however, dropped behind and fired at the unfortunate
creature. A fearful scream was heard, and the next
moment a new-born child fell out of the tree! That
very day the wife and child of this monster, when
crossing the Derwent, in a small boat, were upset by
a sudden squall, and both were drowned, and he himself came to a very violent death not long after.
Their sufferings were of such a character that Dr.
Coke, a gifted writer on the West Indies, says that
" the author who records their miseries will almost be
deemed incredible; and whilst his narrative will be
read with astonishment, it will perhaps be associated
with the marvelous, and consigned to the shelves of
romance."

In 1849 the only survivors of the race were twelve

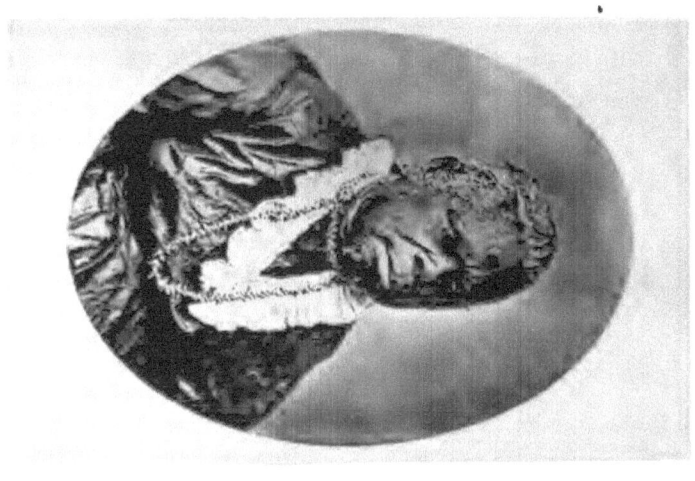

TRUGANINI,
The Last Tasmanian Woman.

WILLIAM LANNAE,
The Last Tasmanian Man.

men and twenty-three women. The government removed them to comfortable quarters near Hobart,
and placed them under the superintendence of a
physician. William Lannae, the last man of the
Tasmanian race, died March 2nd, 1869. One year
before that, when the Duke of Edinburgh visited
Tasmania, he was dressed in a blue suit, with a gold
lace band around his cap. He was introduced to the
Duke, with whom he walked proudly on the grounds
of the Regatta, as if he felt sure that only himself
and the Duke were in possession of royal blood!
Soon after this, he went on a whaling expedition, and
on his return, being paid the wages due, some sixty
dollars, having an ungovernable propensity for beer,
he drank himself to death. On the above date, when
attempting to dress himself, he fell back on his bed —
dead. He was only thirty-four years of age when he
died. His funeral was attended by a large concourse
of people. Before the body was finally consigned to
the tomb, it was discovered that the *head* had been
taken, and what became of it has not been satisfac-
torily made known to the public. The skin had been
taken off it, and drawn over the face of another person who had died about the same time, and whose
head, with Lannae's face, was made to do duty for
poor Lannae's missing head. An eminent physician
was suspended by Government, under strong pre-
sumptive evidence that he had had something to do
with the mutilation. So passed away the last man of a
most cruelly ill-treated race. The rest of the few

under Government care, although there were twelve
men and twenty-three women, all passed away having
no children.   Mr. James Boswick, F. R. G. S., author of " The Last of the Tasmanians," says, in refer-
ence to this: " It seems that to other causes than
violence and disease must be assigned the extinction
of these children of nature, when coming into contact
with the civilized European."   What these *other*
causes may be, I do not know, but I heard a strange-
ly significant remark made by an old settler, as to
what they possibly might be.

The last woman, Truganini, or *Sea Weed*, died
May 8th, 1876, aged sixty years, so that there is not
now a single native Tasmanian living.   After no
small inquiry, I could never find out that more than
just a few persons were every brought under the influence of the gospel. The Bishop of Tasmania, in
his account of them, shows, I think, a more meagre
result that way, than ever came to pass with any
tribe of men whom it was sought to civilize and
Christianize.   I was shown two skulls of aborigines,
their size being some three or four inches-less than
the average European's. When a lighted candle was
introduced into the male skull, the organs of de-
structiveness, secretiveness and amativeness were
seen to be almost transparent. All the higher facul-
ties seem to have been very small. Such, at least,
was the reading of this skull by a phrenologist to me.
But reading the sad facts of their cruel fate, one can
hardly help feeling and seeing that, in their few good

qualities, they often excelled their more highly gifted destroyers, and in their bad or indifferent ones were far oftener exceeded, all the readings of phrenology to the contrary notwithstanding. I spoke with many who had personally known Truganini, and all spoke of her as a bright, cheerful, intelligent woman. They are all gone now, and the whole truth will not be known until that time when " the earth shall no more cover her slain." H. EXLEY.

SYDNEY, New South Wales, Australia, May 13, 1881.

LETTER XII.

INSTEAD of being this moment in London, or at home, I am here in Newtown, Sydney, New South Wales. What may be the Providence and meaning of this, to me, entirely unsought, undesired, and strange journey, from first to last, I know not, but hope and feel assured that it has a divine significance in more directions than one.

Writing from Hobart, Tasmania, in plenty of time, under ordinary circumstances, to secure a berth on the "Orient" for London, I found that, owing to a sudden change in the time of sailing of the mail-boat from Launceston, by the Postmaster General, I could not secure a berth, every one being engaged before I got to Melbourne. Bro. Haley had just received a very pressing letter for evangelistic help from this far-off region, and as I would not leave until two more weeks passed away, it was urged upon me to go to Newtown, Sydney, for two months. Leaving Melbourne on Wednesday, the 13th of April, in the Lyee-moon, after a two days' very stormy, but to me not unpleasant, voyage, I arrived in Sydney at 5 P. M., Friday. Owing to the letter posted at Melbourne not getting to hand until two hours after my arrival,

(140)

no one expected me. All the hotels were full, and, after trying some five or six, I gave it up and took a "'bus" for Newtown, not knowing either a brother, a name, or an address. Arriving in Newtown, at my first inquiry for "Christians," I was directed to the house of one of them, and in a few minutes received a kindly welcome from Bro. J. Kingsbury, Jr. Not, however, until 10 P. M., did I find a resting-place, weary and foot-sore, at the home of Bro. Thomas Hawkins, one of the elders of the church at Newtown, with whom, and his excellent family, I made my home.

The whole distance from the open sea to the city, the bay and harbor are very fine in their exceedingly picturesque beauty, being skirted on either side by bold, high bluffs, broken at short intervals by beautiful inlets and smaller bays — the bluffs at two or three points being crowned with forts and their accompanying instruments of destruction. Nature seems to have done everything necessary to make Sydney harbor and bay at once one of the safest and most capacious and beautiful in the world. The city itself, with everything that can be desired in the way of situation, configuration of country and seaboard, is a spoiled city. With buildings, both public and private, banks, post-office, town-hall, cathedrals, churches, government offices, and business buildings, public library and museum, which no less a word than "magnificent" will describe, and on a scale which excites both wonder and astonishment, it is

none the less a spoiled city. Its streets are so narrow, and often crooked, that the finest buildings are
defrauded of their proper effect by their surroundings.
It seems to be *the* city of fine buildings, narrow
streets, public houses, and *dogs.* It exceeds, I think,
all the places I was ever in for the number of dogs to
be seen, and evidently well kept, for they are a good-
tempered host.

Sydney, with its suburbs, is a vast city, and covers
a very large area. Near to where I am writing, and
about three miles from the city proper, is a closed
cemetery, in which lie buried about 18,000. When
opened, it seems to have been thought that the city
would never push itself out so far; but now a large
population surrounds it, and the suburbs stretch out
for miles beyond it. The same mistake and crime
against the future welfare of this vast city is being
committed in all the out-lying suburbs, of narrow
streets. The streets are crowded with people, intent
on business or pleasure. The cabs, omnibuses, and
steam-car tramways, do an enormous business. Ninety
trains of passenger cars leave and return every day,
engaged in suburban traffic, about six cars to a train,
all made on our American model, but nearly all made
here in Sydney.

On a recent week there were taken 182,589 single
fares on the three steam-tramway lines in the city
itself, all of which belong to and are worked by the
government, and with great advantage to the revenue.
In addition to all this, there is a vast omnibus service,

and running to every corner of the distant suburbs, at the rate of about two cents per mile.

As an indication of the commercial importance of Sydney, I find that there visited the wharfs of this city in 1879 — 1,268,377 tons in shipping. The mineral wealth of the Colony is also very great, but considered as but in the infancy of its development as yet. Up to 1879, about 280 tons of gold had been taken from the mines, in value more than $168,000,-000; the tin, iron and copper swell it up to more than $250,000,000. The entire product of gold in the colonies of New Zealand, Tasmania, Victoria, Queensland and New South Wales, reaches about 2,200 tons. The output of coal, in this colony alone, in 1879, was 1,620,497 tons. Its tin area is 5,440,-000 acres; its iron area, 1,400 square miles, and of copper, 6,713 square miles.

I visited the Agricultural Exhibition which has just closed here; the exhibitors were very few, not nearly so many as may be seen at almost any of our less pretentious Western Exhibitions of a similar character. The exhibits, however, were all of a very superior character. Amongst "Reapers and Self-Binders," the "Wood's," of New York State, took the first prize over McCormick's. The exhibits of cattle and horses, sheep and swine, were all of a quality of which it may be said that they were almost faultless. I attended the succeeding sale of Short-horns and other high-priced cattle, and the prices realized were in every case high. The cattle-owners

and stockmen of this vast colony are fully awake to
the signs and demands of the times, and are improving their herds up to the highest point of perfection
as rapidly as they can. The competition between
them and our Western producers will be keen — but
all will reap the benefit, in a much better article than
is often now to be obtained.

One company here — the Orange Company — has
already entered upon arrangements by which it will
be enabled to send 50,000 carcasses of beef, each
averaging 800 pounds of meat, in the most thoroughly
perfect condition, as far any present known appliances
can secure that, to the London market, yearly. Besides these 40,000,000 pounds of beef, they will also
be able to send 28,000,000 pounds of mutton. Vast
as this amount is, it will hardly furnish two pounds
per head, per annum, to the English population, so
there is an immense field and market to be occupied
and supplied there. Australian meat will command
the first place and the best prices in England, unless
similar conditions are brought about by our farmers
and stockmen. In the slaughtering of the animals,
the most scientific methods are employed, by which
death is instantaneous, and the blood most completely
drained away. The company has also consulted the
leading butchers in England, as to the condition of
meat which best suits the very best English markets,
and are bending all their energies to secure *that*.

They have some thousands of acres of fine grass
lands attached to their establishments, so that all the

cattle, on arriving, are at once put into pasture, remaining there for two or more weeks, and both resting and improving all the time. Not one animal is driven a long distance or brought a long distance on the cars, and then, in its weary and fretted condition, slaughtered, to the great injury of the meat, and consumer also. They are slaughtered when at their best. These are the conditions which will secure the first place in the market. Another thing, also of prime importance: only the choicest animals are sent to slaughter for the English market. The government has put down a side line of rails to their establishment, and has entered into an arrangement by which it agrees to supply them as the need shall be manifested, with refrigerating cars made on the best and most approved plans, so that the meat, when frozen by the company, will be, at the time of shipment, put into chilled cars, from which it will be transferred in specially-constructed *lighters* to the freezing-rooms on the steamer which is to convey it to England. The same company sees to it that so much of the meat as belongs to various owners, is put up carefully in thoroughly clean canvas bags, bearing the brands of their owners. They also are beginning what will soon assume large proportions: wool-washing, fell-mongering and glue-making. There are in this colony more than 37,000 stockholders, owning 360,000 horses, 2,914,210 horned cattle, and 29,043,-211 sheep, at the last stock-taking, in 1879.

The wool of this colony is said to hold a high place

10

in all the wool markets in the world. My brother,
who is quite a connoisseur of wools, has entered into
a contract in this colony to classify the wool, and
superintend the shearing of some 90,000 sheep, and
the washing of the wool.

It is now the middle of June, and they call it
winter. It is certainly now and then a little chilly,
and gets nearly down to freezing, but the fields are
gloriously green, and the orange trees are loaded with
golden yellow fruit, and the hedge-rows are beautiful
with flowers of the tall native Box. I do n't know if
they have such a thing as winter here, unless it is as
everywhere else — the " winter of discontent." I was
visiting a sick lady two days ago, who has been in
this colony fifty years, who told me she had never
seen snow in all that time.

The public parks, gardens, libraries and museums,
are all on a scale which excite astonishment. I
visited the Public Free Library — by no means a
small building, but it was evident, at a glance, that it
was too small for the accommodation of its readers.
Every table was crowded. The government has voted
the means for the erection of an entirely new building, and on a scale, and of such architectural beauty,
as to be quite abreast with the best institutions of its
kind. There is also a free public lending library in
connection with it, and the literature in demand is
fairly represented in the issues from it to the public,
in the following items, which I have obtained by a
personal application to the very courteous Librarian,

Mr. W. W. Palmer, who at once, on my making
known my wishes, took down the books, and copied
out for me himself the sum totals, since the present
year opened, as follows: Number of visitors, 16,650;
number of days open, 144; books issued: Natural
Philosophy and Science, 1938. History, Chronology,
Antiquities and Mythology, 1471. Biography and
Correspondence, 1660. Geography, Topography, Voy-
ages and Travels, 2509. Jurisprudence, 253. Mental and Moral Philosophy, 611. Poetry and the
Drama, 528. Miscellaneous, 12,071. Specifications
of Patents, 1. Total, 21,042. Taking all in all,
there seems to be a very creditable taste for the best
literature amongst the great body of artisans in this
city. Midway between the city and the point where
I am laboring, there is a very large enclosure of land
laid out in fine taste, in which, at various distances,
are situated the State University and the three colleges of the Episcopalians, Presbyterians and Roman
Catholics, all large and very beautiful buildings. On
Lord's days large numbers of people congregate at
various points on the grounds, and earnest preachers
of various denominations are there to preach that
which they believe to be the gospel. Our brethren
are not in any way behindhand in this good work.
Bros. Nelson and Goode, of the Newtown Church, are
here, preaching every Lord's day, when the weather
permits, and it is very rarely the case that it does
not; and Bro. Picton and others are found in the
same work in the Domain, really the Central Park of

Sydney. Some of the brethren also preach in the suburbs every Lord's day evening. In addition to the above colleges, the Wesleyans and the Congregationalists have each their own college in the suburbs, and all, I believe, are well patronized, except the last.

Some earnest Christian men, who have formed themselves into an Aborigines Protection Society, are doing something both to protect and Christianize the black native population in the interior, and to care for the few that are found lingering in and around Sydney. The efforts to Christianize them are meeting with some real success, but the efforts are not at all commensurate with the needs of the case. Those of the natives I have seen are really not bad specimens of physical build, but they are nearly black. They are reported to be very expert in learning the various handicrafts. As trackers they fully rival the clear-eyed red man of the West. Those who have lived among them and near them for many years, assure me that they are intelligent, peaceable and kind, but have often been treated even with cruelty. Bro. W. Newell, a gentleman whom it has been my joy to baptize, and who has lived among them for years, confirms all this. He also tells me he has seen them throw the boomerang in such a way, and with such force and skill, that whilst it was thrown a considerable distance forward, it would come darting and bounding back and far *behind* the place from where it was thrown, and even strike off the upper tier of bricks from a house-chimney. I have also been informed that they throw the spear with such consummate skill and precision that, when in hunting they have come into the presence of game, they form a large circle around it, at a considerable distance, and every man throws his spear at the same instant, and so that the points *always* strike into the ground, with the upper ends converging to a center over the head of the game, thus literally encaging it.

The poisoned arrows used all over these South Sea lands are a terrible weapon. Through the kindness of Bro. Newell, I have received two of these arrows, together with two non-poisoned ones, and a stone-headed spear, but very sharp. The arrows are poisoned by being thrust into a corpse that is far advanced in corruption. It is rarely the case that even a slight injury with one of these does not prove fatal. I also received four fine boat-paddles made from the wood of the cocoa-nut tree, and which are so made as to be used as spears in case of a naval encounter. These were all taken from the natives of the Island of *Rubianno*, one of the Solomon group, by whom, some few months ago, Lieut. Bower and several men of the "Sand-Fly," were so treacherously massacred, whilst the whole of the crew were on shore, except a few. These weapons were taken by the men sent to punish them for their crime, and through the courtesy of Bro. Newell they have come into my possession. During our stay at Wellington, New Zealand, we saw the Sand Fly, still bearing the marks of their savage fury.

We have not many churches in New South Wales.
The principal ones are the churches of Sydney and
Newtown. The church in Sydney has the good
providence of having for its evangelist, Bro. John
Strang, formerly of Glasgow, Scotland, a man loved
and esteemed by all who know him. I have spoken
for him twice: once, by request, on "The Resurrection of Jesus the Christ: Did it ever take place?"
The tea-meeting is an institution here in Sydney, as
in all the Colonies, and it was my pleasure to be an
invited guest to the one recently held in the Sydney
chapel. The membership is about 150, and at least
100 sat down to tea, although it was a wet night,
when nearly $200 was given or promised, every
shilling of which would be paid to effect some needed
repairs and alterations. They seem to have good
hopes for the future; but Sydney is by no means an
easy field. They have a Sunday-school of about
seventy or more scholars, with a sufficient staff of
teachers.

The Newtown church has a membership of about
170. It has two elders, four deacons, about 100
scholars in the Sunday-school, and eleven teachers.
Bro. Hawkins, one of the elders, not only superin-
tends the Sunday-school, but also teaches a Bible-
class one evening in the week; he does his full share
of the teaching, and in the absence of an evangelist
will be found ready to do his share of preaching also.
Being a man engaged in an exacting business all the
week, his labor for the church is not a small matter.

During the time I labored for this church, I took
charge of the Bible-class, and found it a most pleasant
and profitable work, as I spent nearly the whole day
in preparing for the evening lesson.

The two churches own buildings of quite $10,000
value between them, and the churches will seat about
350 or 400 each. Dr. Kingsbury is the other elder
associated with Bro. Hawkins, an earnest, able man,
with a nerve as unflinching as steel, and a heart as
tender as a woman's.

When a boy, he was the subject of one of those
strange providences, which arrest attention, and which
on ordinary grounds seem so difficult to understand.
He and his brother being out one day together, they
found a brace of dueling-pistols, but rusted from ex-
posure. Elated with their treasure-trove, they took
them home, and soon began to fight mock-duels.
Day after day, and week after week, in the house and
everywhere 'round, they made sport in that way. This
was done *hundreds of times.* One day the boys got
up into the topmost room of the house, with a sky-
light opening on to the roof of the house, and the
window of it happened to be open. They played at
their old dueling game again, snapping off their rusty
weapons, with caps, until they were tired, when one
of them observing the open sky-light said, " Now for
a go through the window," and snapped his pistol off
once more; but this time there was a loud report, and
a ball was discharged, which passed through the roof
and inside boards of the next house. This led to a

thorough examination of the other pistol, and it also
was found to contain a ball. The pistols had been
snapped off with caps many hundreds of times by the
boys at each other, when this "Now for a go through
the window" revealed the fact that they had been
playing with death all the time, and only by one of
those mysterious providences which take place so
often, was this last snapping-off of the pistol turned
away from the breast of the brother and aimed
through the open sky-light.

Bro. Kingsbury is getting far on now, on the road
to the valley of the shadow, but he seems as if the
light of the city came streaming upon him, and with
him it may be said, "*At evening time there is light.*"

Since coming here my meetings have been really
good, and the interest apparently of a very serious
nature. It has been my privilege, under God, to
help to reap after the sowing of others. Thirteen
have confessed the Saviour's name since I began my
labors amongst them, ten of whom I have baptized;
the rest will be baptized in a few days, and probably
more also. One Lord's day I went to the large suburban town of Parramatta, and preached for the
Baptists and their congregation, accompanied by Bro.
Picton, who goes there once in two weeks. They
seem to be drawing nearer to Apostolic lines, and
hope is entertained that an entire return will be the
result. In the afternoon of the same Lord's day I
went to the Poor-house, and preached to a large company of the aged sick, lame and blind. It was good

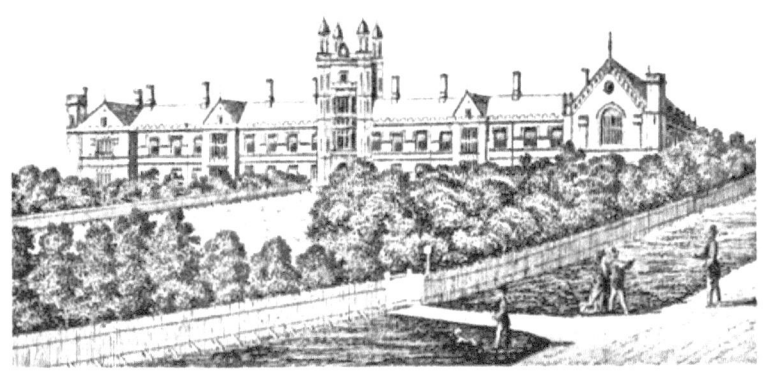

THE UNIVERSITY.

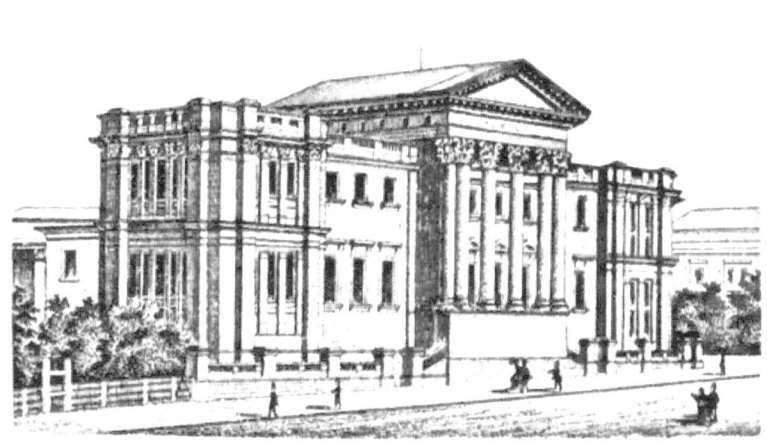

THE MUSEUM.

to be there. One poor fellow, blind for the past ten
years, sat on his bed, with a face almost illuminated,
as if the light in fading from the eyes had passed into
his countenance. It was a beautiful testimony to the
ennobling and redeeming power of the gospel, to see
some of the young members of the Baptist Church
there (and they visit this and other similar institutions
every Lord's day afternoon), to preach Jesus and to
speak comforting words to the aged and sick. If the
young men and women of our churches, in cities
where this kind of work can be done, were to set
about it, what a blessed influence would be created. I
felt it a privilege thus to be permitted to try and
press some cup of consolation to lips parched with the
agony of many of this world's dark Gethsemanes.
On one Lord's day morning I visited a little "church
in the house" of Bro. Stimpson, at Fairfield, also in
the suburbs, where for the past twenty years, with
hardly an exception, but when the weather has rendered it impossible, the few brethren and sisters have
met to break the commemorative loaf. It is about as
isolated a place as we often have in the West, but the
church does not fail to remember its Lord.

In one hour the mail for San Francisco closes, and
I must also close this letter, to be in time. This is
the last letter from this region, as I have engaged a
berth on the *John Elder* for London, and expect to
leave here at 5 P. M., June 24. In eight days I shall
be on the sea, and, going *via* Melbourne and Adelaide,
expect to see once more Bros. Haley, Bates, Gore and

others. When this reaches the *Standard* I shall be, I suppose, on the Red Sea, and by the middle of September I trust to be once more in my own far Western home. The more I see of these Colonies, the more does it become evident that they are destined to fill a high place in the affairs of this world. I am profoundly thankful I have been permitted to see them in part, and that my visit and Bro. Coop's will not be in vain. It seem to me a great misfortune. that all the churches of Christ in America, Great Britain, and these Colonies, have not a more intimate acquaintance with each other, for mutual encouragement and common work.

I have now done for this time, but will write once more, if anything of sufficient interest calls for it. Till then I lay down my pen, and now go to other work again for the few days which yet remain.

H. EXLEY.

NEWTOWN, SYDNEY, New South Wales, June 16, 1881.

LETTER XIII.

IT WAS the doctrine of Dr. Thomas, long years ago, if my memory is correct, that Christianity was the religion of civilized man only, and that we must wait for civilization to become the pioneer for the religion of the cross. How greatly the leaven of this pitiless doctrine, taught by many, may have retarded the missionary spirit amongst us, is not easy to say; but certain it is, the logic of facts teaches quite another thing. Over all these South Sea lands it has been the experience of all who have sought to begin from the side of trying to civilize them first, that the only way in which civilization could come to the savage was to *first Christianize him*, and then his civilization speedily followed, and that without any special effort. Rev. J. Ingliss, himself a missionary, and entitled to speak with authority, said years ago: "Indeed, it is clear as day, that it is only so far as Christianity is extended that commercial and scientific objects can be attained in these islands. It is only Christianity that brings security to life and property, and develops the industry of the natives and the resources of the islands." To look upon the pictures, placed side by side, of the Christianized native and the unchristian-

(155)

ized one, at once shows the elevating power of the gospel.

In 1810, or even later, there was not in all the Pacific islands a single Polynesian who could read a single word; nor was there a single printed word in any one of their languages. Fifty years after that, and what do we see? There is seen sailing, on her way to England, the missionary barque, the *John Williams*, and carrying on board the Rev. G. Turner, with a corrected copy of the entire Bible, with marginal references, for a *second edition*, to be printed in the Samoan language; the Rev. G. Gill, with a corrected copy of the entire Raratonga Bible, for a *third edition*, also with marginal references; and had it not been for the illness of another missionary, the Rev. A. Chisholm would have been on the same barque, with a corrected copy of the entire Bible, also with marginal references, for a *third edition*, in the Tahitian language; whilst the Rev. J. Ingliss, from whose pen I have gleaned these facts, was on the same vessel, with a complete translation of the whole New Testament, to be printed in the Aneityam language. Since man wandered away from God, as he well asks: " Was there any single ship ever freighted with three translations of the entire Bible, and a fourth, of the New Testament, to be printed?" What a wonderful commentary on the prediction of Isaiah: " He shall not fail, nor be discouraged, till He have set judgment in the earth, and the isles shall wait for his law." What a wealth of love and compassion was here laid at the Redeemer's feet, outweighing any gift of thousands of silver and gold, that so in some measure He might "see of the travail of his soul and be satisfied." Besides these, many other books, in important departments of knowledge, have been translated and printed in Polynesian tongues, and what is wonderful in itself, *every word* of these languages had, in great measure, to be caught as it floated rapidly, and often indistinctly, from the lips of the speaker, and the meaning of the word, and the whole structure of the language in which it had a place, mastered, before the missionary could begin to teach at all.

The world has no grander or nobler heroes on all its manifold rolls of honor, than such men as these. Their motto was: "We can not stoop too low to save." I heard one of our own brethren in New Zealand, Bro. Caleb Wallis, make the remark, during conversation with myself and Bro. Coop, "I believe in going down into the gutter to save men." The man who does not, has small business to think that he is an imitator of the Son of God. The almost incredible ignorance, filth, cruelty, superstition and cannibalism, with all that the first chapter of Romans alleges of the heathen world of that age, which met the missionary everywhere, and through which he had to toil, shut off from all society, an exile from home and all that makes home so precious, in constant peril of his life — all this demanded men and *women* for the work than whom heaven itself could not find nobler.

Sixty years ago the shipwrecked sailor or passenger, thrown on these shores, had not the least security for his life longer than the time he could hide himself.

Even after large progress had been made on many of the islands, the missionary himself has fallen a martyr in his work, to the savage revenge of the natives, in retaliation for outrages inflicted on them by traders, who, whether they believed that Christianity was only for civilized man or not, did not believe in it for themselves.

The ignorance met with by the missionaries, is amusing, as well as sad. Rev. S. Taplin, missionary in South Australia, says that when he went among them the natives told him that twenty years before, when they for the first time saw a white man on horseback, they thought that the horse was the white man's mother, because he was carried on its back; and another tribe, the first time they saw pack-bullocks, thought they were the white fellows' wives, because they carried the baggage. Their ideas concerning the origin of their different languages, are just as nonsensical. They attribute them to the death of an ill-tempered old woman, who, when living, used to go about and, with a stick she always carried, scatter the fires around which others were sleeping. Men and women came from different places to rejoice over her death, and then fell to eating the body, when each company, as in succession they shared in the feast, at once began speaking in another and different tongue from all the rest. Once, when speaking to an

old woman, he said, "We shall die, and so will you."
She replied, "We shall *die?* Then let us eat plenty
of flour." So said the Greek and Roman : "Let us
eat and drink, for to-morrow we die."

The *kind* of work the missionary has had to do in
New Zealand and Australia, and to do which work he
bent all his soul, was and is a very different thing
from going on a mission to England, or other civilized land, where he is not only abundantly well sustained, but surrounded by friends and peace, safety
and civilization, and with the means of a varied
culture within his reach but seldom or never within
his reach at home. To talk about self-sacrifice in
their case, by the side of missions in New Zealand, or
other of the vast number of the Polynesian isles,
is an abuse of terms. In comparison with this work,
theirs is nothing more than a real pleasure trip, and is
as unlike the work to be done in these far-off lands, as
is the rest and safety, and home comfort, and luxury,
and manifold blessings, which fill the most favored
homes to-day, to the hunger and cold, and suffering
and struggles of the forefathers of the Revolution.

The kind of work the missionary had to do — besides shutting himself off from all civilization nearly,
and living in the midst of peril all the time, but
intensely alive and active to catch every floating
word and unravel its meaning — was to learn the
great lesson of the Master in all its fullness of meaning; and at times, in very deed, both the missionary
and his gentle but courageous helpmeet, girded them-

selves with towels, to do more than wash the disciples' feet! One of the new converts of Mr. Taplin,
a fine young man, having set himself to wash off the
grease and red ochre, which it had perhaps taken
months to plaster on, succeeded pretty well with his
body; but when it came to his head, he failed utterly,
and went seeking for help to the mission house. Mrs.
Taplin at once, with her servant girl, set to work,
and getting a tub of hot water, and soap, scrubbed
till the stuff was cleaned away, and his really fine,
curly locks shone again in their original brightness.
The annals of missions abound in such work. Sometimes the congregations gathered into the mission
stations are dressed out in the strangest and most gro-
tesque style. Mark Twain never imagined anything
more ridiculous than in mission stations is only realest fact. Some go dressed in the common opossum
rug; others, in a double blanket, gathered on a stout
string, and hung around the neck like a cloak; others,
with nothing on but a blue shirt, and others again
with only a woman's skirt or petticoat, with the waist
of it around the neck, and one arm through a hole at
the side. Mr. Taplin tells that, one Lord's day, a
tall savage walked into the mission school, and grave-
ly sat down, with nothing on at all except a high-
crowned hat and a waistcoat!

To undertake the redemption of such as these,
surely demands the noblest, the bravest, and the most
Christ-loving, soul-loving, and self-sacrificing men
and women the churches have in them. Where

others would become digusted, then wholly discouraged, and then ignominiously leave the work because
they feel their own respectability insulted — or that
the work is too unclean for them to touch it — these
see in all these dreadful signs, so many additional
reasons to seek to save. Nor are such required in the
work, in any place on earth, whose sympathies with
the redeeming Christ, and the Christ-work that needs
to be done, are so small — as I heard of one expressing
it — that they "would rather live and die slaves in
their native land," than be anything possible within
the gift of other lands. All such as these have no
business to leave their homes. The work of missions
requires men and women so consecrated to Christ that
they will go with their lives in their hands, as the
common saying has it, and go to live and die in it,
but not to give it up.

The Episcopalian Church of England, with all her
faults, has given some notable examples of what a
missionary should be, both in New Zealand and over
a large number of other islands. Bishop Selwyn and
Bishop Coleridge Patteson, son of the Right Hon.
Judge Patteson, whose family has given some of the
most accomplished judges to the English bench, and
who on his mother's side was very nearly related to
Samuel Taylor Coleridge — these men, reared in the
lap of luxury and refinement, yet gave themselves up
to the work of missions in a manner and with a spirit
impossible to any not entirely under the masterhood
of the gospel.

11

Bishop Patteson, after having given up all within his reach at home, and when, in the midst of the most trying work, he had taken fair measure of all, wrote, and in the tenderest words, thanked his father for giving him up to the work. He said: "*It has made me more of a man; I am in my right place.*" He was content to live in one large room, built of the kauri pine, with no furniture in it except a bedstead, a writing-desk and an old book-case; to clean out his own room, make his own bed, and to help clean away the things from the table after meals. Yet he was calm and happy, and though thoughts of home were constantly flitting before his mind, he wrote home: " I like the natives in the school very much. The regular wild, untamed fellow is not so pleasant at first. Dirty, always smoking, a mass of double blanket, his wigwam sort of place filthy, his food ditto; but then he is probably intelligent, and not insensible to the advantage of hearing about religion." Religious teaching is the very smallest part of the hard work that has to be done, and he writes: "and the difficulty is to do for them what parents have to do for their children, not only in assisting them, but descending to the smallest matters, washing, scrubbing, sweeping, and all the acts of personal cleanliness." He writes home and tells his friends that the missionary needs to be a carpenter, mason, butcher, and very much of a cook, as well as something of a glazier, and a tinker, to mend his own kettle and saucepan. In visiting, perhaps as many as eighty of the various islands, in company with Bishop Selwyn, it often happened that their little vessel could not get in shore, for the reef or the surf. When such was the case, they would simply take off their coats, and, taking what tools they needed for work in their hands, plunge into the sea, and in peril of life in the sea and on the shore, swim to the land.

Again writing to his father, he points out what kind of a man the missionary must be, so well that I place it here, that every missionary we have now, or may have, who shall read it, will, I hope, be taught by it, for there is abundant need for it: " *The missionary must denationalize himself, and eliminate all that belongs to him as English,* and not as Christian, and he himself not shrinking from the most repulsive offices, even to carrying out the dead silently at night, lest others should see and be alarmed."

Bishop Selwyn would navigate his own vessel, steer it, if need be, live on the same food as his sailors, and lie on the floor of his cabin for weeks, that a sick native might have his bed, and he have the joy of restoring him to health and to his friends. Thus they toiled and lived, until at last Bishop Patteson, going on shore on his errand of mercy, at Nakapii, one of the Santa Cruz islands, was martyred in his work, when the villainy of white traders had just outraged the natives in abducting five of them away. This was as recently as 1871. His body was brought off from the shore immediately, wrapped in a native mat, with a palm leaf covering the breast.

The first missionaries to New Zealand went there
when it was a land of savages, feasting on human
flesh, drinking human blood, and that for days together. From the pen of one of these, I find the
following : "Scenes like this we have often seen. My
dear partner has been on the mission station, with the
wives of other missionaries, when on one morning as
many as eleven men have been murdered, cooked and
eaten, within sight of the missionary house. I was
in the midst of them alone (yet not alone, for God
was with me to protect me) while the bodies and
hatchets of the murderers were still wet with the
blood of these slain, and while they were preparing
ovens for the bodies of the victims. They danced
round me, and when they had concluded their repast,
I preached to them." " I have heard of as many as
thirteen children being cooked in one oven made of
heated stones." How marvelous the power of the
gospel! Some of these became both humble Christians and preachers of the gospel. Much more could
I say, but these facts are enough. Heathen missions
are calling upon us now for our share in the glorious
work, and the question presses for answer :

> " Shall we whose souls are lighted
> With wisdom from on high,
> Shall we, to man benighted,
> The lamp of life deny?"

But missions cost money. You who, at home, have
all you have as the fruit of missions of a long past

age, you are called upon to bring some offering, and lay it as your tribute at the feet of the Redeemer — some precious jewel wherewith to adorn the Redeemer's crown, and help to swell the "*satisfaction*" of that great heart which was broken on the cross. What shall it be? Don't forget that the Great Arbiter himself has stated it, the talent that is forfeited is the one that has been withheld. Amongst the "books opened" in that day, will be the Book of Missions — and the Book of the Church!

Let none offer to go, let none be sent, but such as are ready, in the presence of the cross, to lay all at His feet. There is no romance in heathen missions: the work is stern and all self-sacrificing, from first to last. To lay it down because of the deep degradation of those it is sought to save, is evidence both of ignorance of the true spirit of missions, and of utter unfitness for the work.

> "For whoso loves the Lord aright
>   No soul of man can worthless find.
> *All* will be precious in his sight,
>   For Christ on *all* hath shined."

The more utter the lostness of the heathen, the greater the need for that nobleness which "counts all things but loss," that Christ may have the "dominion from sea to sea, and from the rivers to the ends of the earth." The greater the difficulties, the more need to say with St. Xavier, Romanist though he was, when friends tried to dissuade him from undertaking mis-

sionary work, by spreading before him the dangers to
be encountered :

> "Hush you!   Close your dismal story.
> What to me are tempests wild ?
> Heroes on their way to glory
> Mind not pastime for a child.
> 'Tis for *souls of men* I 'm sailing!
> Blow ye winds, north, south, east, west.
> Though the storms be round me wailing,
> There 'll be calm within my breast."

The glory to be won by those who go in the true
spirit of missions, in the "ages to come," is only to
be measured by the brightness of the firmament — of
the stars, and of the sun, and it shall endure forever.

There are *missionary crowns* still to be won.   Who
will enter the lists to win?   Who can reckon the
fullness of the joy of those *who have sent* forth laborers, and of the *laborers* who shall go, when in the
great reaping-day, they both shall see that "their
labor has not been in vain"?   H. EXLEY.

LETTER XIV.

HAVING now sailed over so many seas, and visited so many of these lands of the great Pacific, and having seen so much that is wonderful and beautiful also, it may not be amiss to group together a number of things in themselves of real interest, gathered from many sources — but all sources of highest worth* — for a better appreciation of what has been seen; and to put them within as small compass as may be.

Strangers, indeed, we were, coming to these oldest of all lands, with but small idea of what they would be like, but perhaps, on that very account, the strangeness and newness of everything we saw "lent enchantment to the view." Until the gospel visited, and with its "light of life" lifted off at least some of the darkness, it was truly to be said of them all that they were lands

> " Where every prospect pleases,
> And only man is vile."

As we sailed over these deep seas, in sight and alongside of, as well as visiting many of their shores,

---

* For most of the facts in this, and the last letter, which did not come under personal observation, the authors quoted from are in every instance men of emiuence, as ministers, missionaries, historians, etc. — H. E.

from San Francisco to New Zealand and Australia, we were constantly impressed with the idea that we were journeying in regions where nature appears at her best. Lofty mountains covered with forests, and lesser hills clothed in fadeless green, extinct vol-canoes, and towering peaks, often seeming to stretch themselves up to the sky, as seen from a distance at sea, and scarcely to be distinguished from the white, fleecy clouds of heaven, as their snow-covered sum-mits mingled with them; castellated rocks rising up from the depths, and lifting their heads as if they were the appointed priests to offer up to heaven the gathered incense of earth and sea, reminded one of Coleridge's hymn to the sunrise in the vale of Cham-ouni, and his lofty address to Mont Blanc:

> Rise, oh! ever rise;
> Rise, like a cloud of incense from the earth!
> Thou kingly spirit, throned among the hills,
> Thou dread ambassador from earth to heaven.
> Great hierarch! tell thou the silent sky,
> And tell the stars and tell yon rising sun,
> Earth, with her ten thousand voices, praises God.

The sea itself filled with the strangest and most antique forms of fish-life; the sky, wondrously clear by day, at night is suffused with a soft and universal glory, streaming from countless stars which stud it over all its vast expanse; the solemn depths all around us, and a silence in harmony with all that is grand in earth, sea and sky — one had but to forget for a moment that " the dark habitations of cruelty "

were around us also, to imagine that we had reached
almost to the gates of " Paradise Regained."

The depth of all these seas, from San Francisco to
Australia, whilst easily expressed in numbers, is
almost beyond the power of the mind to grasp.
From San Francisco to Honolulu, the average depth
is about 12,000 feet; from the Sandwich Islands to
New Zealand, about 18,000 feet, and from New Zealand to Australia, 16,000 feet; so that these vast
bodies of water rest upon, and some of these lands
rise up above, one of the areas of deepest depression
in the world.

New Zealand, rising from such a profound depth, is
said to furnish in its vegetation, but more especially
in its bird-life, the strongest claim to be considered
the oldest of all lands above the face of the deep to-
day; and that it is not, as is frequently supposed, but
the last remains of a continent, now submerged to
such a depth.

The bird-life of New Zealand is said to carry us
back to a time when as yet the sea rolled over where
Great Britain now rises above its waters, and when
the chalk of its southern area was not deposited.

Active volcanic forces are still at work, and shocks
of earthquakes are of frequent occurrence, one slight
shock taking place while we were there. Over many
parts of New Zealand, craters of volcanoes, both
active and extinct, are found, with boiling lakes,
mud-pools, boiling springs and sulphur deposits. The
Waikato region is especially remarkable for its boil-

ing lakes, mud-pools and springs, and for its magnificent scenery, hardly to be surpassed by any in the
world. It was our misfortune to be so limited in
time that we could only *hear* of all this, and could
not go to see. Volcanic action is so constant and
powerful that, on the coast-line, upheavals and raised
beaches are of frequent occurrence. Only lately, on
one of the coasts, and for a considerable distance,
both along the shore and out to the sea, such an un-
usual commotion, with discoloration of the water, was
seen, that captains of steamers gave it a wide berth.
A vessel that was stranded on one of its coasts in
1814, thirty-five years later was found 200 yards
above high-water mark, and with a tree growing
through the bottom. If scientific conjecture may be
trusted, it is likely true that here man stands on the
oldest surface of the globe above the waters of the
deep; and is still surrounded by some of the most
antique forms of *bird*-life, at least.

It is an interesting fact that whilst the climate
and general character of these islands are highly
favorable to the existence of the serpent race, yet no
snake of any kind is to be found in them. The same,
it is said, is also true of the Sandwich Islands. Can
there be something in the nature of active volcanic
forces, and too strongly influential in the soil to
allow of their existence? Their absence is taken as
proof that New Zealand never formed a part of Australia, as some conjecture, as in that case some forms
of serpent-life which abound in the latter country,

would be found here. We were told by a gentleman
at Dunedin, when talking about this peculiar feature,
that at one time quite a large number of frogs had
been imported, but that every one had died. We did
not think of it in time to inquire if any, either
of frogs or snakes, kept in museums or gardens, managed to escape the influence which has kept the country clear of them all.

Man himself does not seem to have lived on these
islands beyond a few centuries back; not even the
first comers — short, black-skinned, woolly-haired
savages — some relics of whom are yet found in the
Southern island. There was no lion, or tiger, or even
wolf, in the forest, and no serpent in the glade, to
molest him — his only foe was his brother savage.
The tall, straight-haired, muscular Maorie, did not
reach the islands until some time after him. They
hunted the Moa (*Dinornis elephantopus*), a bird with
nothing whatever in the shape of wings, but round-
bodied, with massive legs, and its head stretching
sixteen feet above the ground. We saw one or two
fossil specimens of this giant among birds, in the
museum. There are still found ground-ovens, in
which these first possessors of these islands prepared
their feasts. In some of them, the large bones of
these wingless birds are found, often partially burnt,
and mingled with them the bones of human victims
also — some of the bones of the birds seemingly so
fresh, that they might have been living almost within the last half-century. Dr. Tristram, Canon of

Durham, England, in a series of papers on these interesting matters, says that a few years ago he received a number of bones from one of these ground-
ovens — bones of various birds, and amongst them
bones of at least three young children. It almost
makes one to tremble, as he thinks of the dreadful
ages of darkness, cruelty and blood, which have over-
shadowed all these fair lands, and from which many of
them have not yet emerged.

One fact, discovered some years ago, is considered
pretty conclusive evidence that the *Maorie* made his
advent into New Zealand before these giant birds,
the *Moa*, had passed away. A Maorie skeleton was
found in a cave, in a sitting posture, holding in his
hand an entire egg of the Moa, a small hole pierced
in one end, and held just under the chin, supposed to
be placed there to afford him sustenance, on his way
to or in the land of spirits. Rev. R. Taylor, said by
Canon Tristram to be probably better acquainted with
Maorie history and tradition than any other European, collected many of the native songs, which were
written out by the collector more than twenty years
before colonization began, and which relate to the
skill and prowess of the Maorie in hunting the gigantic Moa. In 1849, when Raupahara, a great native
chief, was buried, the one solitary feather, said to be
the last relic of the bird possessed by the tribe, was
buried with him.

The presence of the Maories does not appear to
date back beyond some six hundred years at most.

Rev. R. Taylor says he perused the genealogy of one
of their noble families, and it gave about twenty-
seven generations from the time of their landing in
New Zealand, and that they have even preserved the
names of the canoes in which they arrived. Their
legends tell how they left the Sandwich Islands, in a
fleet of canoes, about 600 years since, but halting for
some three generations on the road, at the Society or
Friendly Islands, until the land became too strait for
them, provisions were scanty, and a new emigration
was compelled; but taking with them various tropical
plants, such as the sweet-potato, and which will not
grow in New Zealand without artificial cultivation.
Their language is also said to be proof of their de-
scent from the Sandwich Islanders.

There are still here forms of life which in our
Northern hemisphere are only found in a fossil state;
and so, whilst New Zealand is conjectured to be the
oldest of all lands, and its forms of life the most
ancient, it is also conjectured that Australia, with its
wonderful tribes of Marsupials, its Saurians, serpents
and strange fishes, stands next.

Tasmania, only some twenty-four hours' sail from
Australia, and separated by only a shallow sea, in its
natural history is strictly Australian, not having so
much as one peculiar genus of birds different from
Australia. Even the Emu, of which we saw living
specimens in the gardens of Melbourne and Adelaide,
has but recently been exterminated in Tasmania, and
it was identical with the Emu of South Australia. All

this is taken to mean that, at some past time, *Tasmania* formed a part of the Australian main-land.

There are at least two ferocious wild animals peculiar to Tasmania — the Tasmanian tiger, or wild-cat, many of them still found inhabiting the mountains, and which stands almost as high as a greyhound; this and the equally savage beast, the Tasmanian devil, are also Marsupials. We saw fine specimens of each in the Zoölogical Gardens at Melbourne. One of the brethren playfully said to me, when I was about to go to Tasmania, " Don't you think you had better be careful in going there? You know that they have the *devil* there?" To whom I replied, " So long as they keep him safely in the Melbourne gardens, I need not fear him much."

The Fern Trees, of both Tasmania and New Zealand, are marvelous affairs. We saw many on the lands of Bro. C. Wallis. They grow up like any other tree; but all that we saw were at least from six to ten inches in diameter. At about six feet from the ground they put out scores of shoots, each one of which goes straight up, but clinging closely to the central stem, and then puts out long, beautiful fronds, stretching out for many feet, and forming a most delightful shade. In South Australia, the Fern Tree (*Todea Africana*) is often five to six feet in circumference. I saw many in Tasmania, probably very much more than 100 years old, and which, if lifted out of the ground, would weigh much more than 2000 lbs. It is said they will bear transplanting, even the largest ones, to almost any temperate climate in the world.

Tasmanian sea-coasts are especially rich in sea-weeds, not less than 300 varieties having been already classified. Their forms, and almost endless variety in tints and colors, are, I think, if anything, more beautiful than any land weeds or mosses whatever. They seem to say to us,

> " Call us not weeds, we are ocean's gay flowers,
>   For delicate, beautiful, and bright-tinted are we ;
>   Not gently reared either in gardens or bowers,
>   We are rocked by the storms, we are nursed in the sea."

Passing from New Zealand and Tasmania to Australia, the strangest forms of animal life are found, the like of which are not found elsewhere in the world. Not less than 102 species of Marsupials are found, and three Monotremes. The Marsupials have not a single ally or representative elsewhere, save the solitary exception of the American opossum. The *duck-billed platypus* and the *spiny ant-eater* " stand utterly alone, separated by an unbridged chasm from every other quadruped." " Their intestinal parts, resemble those of birds. They have no teeth, nor anything in the place of teeth ; no internal ears, no teats, no placenta, no Marsupial pouch, and have a merrythought like a bird. They have, however, organs which secrete milk." All these are regarded as amongst the very first forms, or relics of the very first, of Mammalian life created on earth.

The bone-caves of Australia have revealed the existence, in times very far remote, of Marsupial lions and bears, which preyed on gigantic *herbivorous* kangaroos, one of which had a skull three feet in length and equal in size to that of the rhinoceros or hippopotamus, whilst the carnassial tooth of its enemy was double the size of that of a modern lion.

Kangaroos still abound, and in large numbers are often hunted down. During my stay in Sydney, I read in the papers of two great kangaroo hunts — in one of them, 200 horses, with their riders, some of them *ladies,* took part in chasing down 500 kangaroos; and in the other, 100 horses, with their riders, hunted down 200 kangaroos. The largest of them weighed about 200 pounds each; but some that we saw in the gardens, of quite that weight, seemed to leap, using, of course, only their hind legs and long tail, as if it was about as easy for them to do it as to nibble at the grass on which they were feeding. When alarmed and escaping from their pursuers, they will leap as much as fifteen feet at a bound, and keep it up for several miles, scarcely varying in the length of each leap, more than an inch or two. Hunted thus, it will not be long before they are very scarce.

The bird-life of Australia is also unlike what is found anywhere else. Of its 630 species, not more than one-thirtieth occur elsewhere, not even in India, a country so close at hand.

Amongst the insects of South Australia, the white ant is a formidable pest. It builds its hill, often, to

a hight of more than twenty-five feet, and from six
to ten feet in diameter, and so strongly as to resist
the heavy tropical rains; the larger ones supposed to
be some hundreds of years old. There are hundreds
of thousands of such hills in the South Australian
Colony. Nothing seems to resist its ravages, short of
sheet-iron. Another curious insect, and very destructive to the timber, is called the *"borer,"* and is about
the size of a common house-fly. On its head it
carries a kind of auger, which, with considerable
force, it strikes into the timber, and then perform-
ing a series of rapid revolutions, perhaps a thousand
in a minute, bores a hole as neatly as any carpenter
could do it.

Some of the trees of Australia will rival the giant
trees of California. In Western Australia, and Tasmania also, the *Eucalyptus globulus* reaches a hight of
300 feet, and the *Eucalyptus collosa*, of Western
Australia, 400 feet; whilst a fallen tree of the *Eucalyptus amygdalina*, in the Dandenong Mountains,
Victoria, measured 420 feet in length.

We saw occasionally hedges of Cactus, and the
flower crowning a stem at least twenty-five feet above
the ground. We saw climbing plants, reaching to
the tops of trees, and coiling round the branches, and
grasping them with something like the grip of death;
and on other trees, enormous masses of parasitical
growths, quite as much on single trees as would fill a
wagon box, and growing at the point where the
branch unites with the main stem, and apparently
12

without either roots or soil, with nothing but air, light and moisture. One of these especially attracted attention: its leaves were so large and broad and curiously formed, and so like the antlers of the deer, that it is called the "stag-horn fern."

The snakes of Australia are numerous, and many of them very poisonous; and the waters on all the coasts abound in the most antique forms of fish-life. The *octopus* is often caught; but not of very large size. I saw three which had been just caught, their arms from one to three feet in length, and quite capable of drowning an incautious bather. We used one as *bait*, when fishing, cutting it into small pieces, and we found it quite tough and leathery, even for a sharp knife. Sharks are very abundant in all these seas, and often of very large size. When standing with Bro. Thos. Magarey at the end of the jetty at Glenelg, two boys who were fishing with rod and line had caught over forty young sharks, and the evening before over thirty, each of them several inches long. Wherever we went, whether on land or on the sea, we were in the midst of wonders aquatic or terrestrial, which incessantly proclaimed—

"Earth with her ten thousand voices praises God."

Now that they have passed away from actual sight, many of the scenes through which we passed seem to have "sunk like gentle rain into the heart, and the memory of them abides as a very precious possession." The quiet beauty of the fruitful field, the rugged grandeur of the snow-mantled, cloud-piercing mountain hight, the wild gloom of the rocky gorge, and the mysterious voice of the solemn sea, as it beats in ceaseless pulsations on the rocky shore; all alike proclaim that God is in all, and that "He made the sea, and the dry land also."

As in thought we stand, again gazing at the four bright stars which form the Southern Cross, and beneath whose glorious light all these strange lands have so long "sat in darkness," and have "dwelt in the shadow of death," we are made to long for the coming of the time when for all of them it shall be true to the uttermost: "Upon them hath the light shined," and that they have turned to "seek Him that maketh the seven stars and Orion, *and turneth the shadow of death into the morning;*" so that when the King comes the second time, He shall be welcomed with the shouts of nations redeemed, and, as it were, carried in triumph to His universal throne, by ransomed multitudes from these far-off "isles of the sea;" and then the ransomed earth and the sobbing sea shall alike share in the joy of creation delivered, and the redemption song shall be sung, "Now is come salvation; now is come the kingdom of our God, and the power of His Christ, and He shall reign forever and forever." H. EXLEY.

LETTER XV.

INDIAN OCEAN,
Lat. 32° 56′ South, } July 7, 1881.
Long. 111° 24′ East,

As CAN be seen from date and place, I am once more on the bosom of the great deep. It is now thirteen days since our stately ship, the *John Elder*, of the *Orient* line of steamers, left Sydney, New South Wales, and for fully twelve days of that time it has been one unbroken storm, fierce head-winds prevailing all the time. Our vessel is one of the largest afloat, being 435 feet in length, and about forty-two in width of beam, and of far more than 4,000 tons burthen, yet it is wonderful how easily this huge piece of naval architecture is lifted and tossed and rocked to and fro by the waves. Great waves, foam-crested, and traveling with a swiftness that is astonishing to behold, like regiments of white-helmeted war troopers in line of battle rushing to the charge, have unceasingly beaten upon us, as if determined that our journey should be as comfortless as possible. We are now, however, clear of the great Australian Bight and its storms, and have fairly entered upon the Indian Ocean, having sailed nearly

3,000 miles since leaving Sydney, and with a journey
of some 10,000 miles yet before us. The visit of
Bro. Coop and myself to these Colonies is now a
thing of the past, but its memories will last on into
the world where all

> " Sweet friendships glow,
> Ceaselessly, forever."

To myself, the journey, with all its providences,
mercies, and precious friendships formed, and all its
opportunities for preaching Christ, has been, and is
to me, a wonderful thing, having never either desired
it, or sought it in any way or manner. Its meaning
the future will best reveal. I started on the long
journey with the understanding that it might be a
journey around the world; and to carry out that possibility I have preferred to return home *via* London,
instead of San Francisco.

At the earnest representations of Bros. Haley and
Gore, whom I met in Melbourne, I was induced to
visit Newtown, Sydney, to try and help the church
there, which had just lost the services of Bro. Lewes,
who had gone to Auckland, New Zealand. I am
thankful and glad that I went. During the ten
weeks I spent at Newtown, *sixteen* were led to put on
Christ by a personal self-yielding to him, and in the
way of his own appointing; others awakened, and a
few were received by letter. The congregations from
the first grew larger, until the church was almost
filled. I am glad also to say that my leaving them

was a deep regret to all. One little incident at the
beginning of my visit seemed likely to terminate it
before it had well begun. The report had preceded
me that Bro. Exley was an *Open Communionist!* Two
or three good brethren waited upon me to ascertain if
this was true. I at once told them that *it was not
true*, and at the same time said I felt hurt that any
calling themselves brethren should so misrepresent
me, and that as I had not sought to come and labor
amongst them, but was urged to come to them in
their pressing need of help, I preferred to take the
next ship and start for home, rather than to be subjected to any unpleasantness on that question. I told
them frankly that, whilst I was not in any way a believer in the unimmersed breaking bread at the Lord's
table, and had not once in all my life-time ever
uttered a word at the Lord's table which could lead
any one unbaptized to break bread, yet that I would
not withdraw the bread or the cup from any known
believer, but unbaptized, who, uninvited, took them
unoffered as they passed along. This was abundantly
satisfactory; for whilst the brethren of Newtown seek
earnestly to·be faithful to the Lord in all things, they
are neither needlessly heresy-hunters nor believers in
constructive treason. It is a good thing, when the
"logic of the head" is not "heady," but wedded to
that loving "logic of the heart" which "thinketh no
evil," and refuses to push to an unrighteous conclu-
sion the positions of others. The Newtown church
has mastered this logic. When in England last, I

was asked by two persons if, unbaptized, they could break bread; to whom I answered that such was not the law of the Lord Jesus. That is my position. I afterwards baptized them both.

My stay in Newtown was rendered very pleasant. Several little excursions were organized, to either go a-fishing or to visit one or other of the many bays near the city.

On one of our fishing trips, we caught a very rare kind of fish, the local name for which is " Box Fish." It was about fifteen inches long, and fully the same in girth, but completely *armour-plated* from just behind the head to within about two inches from the tail, which had thus perfect liberty of action in all its movements. When caught, the hard, bony substance was quite variegated in color, and the colors bright; but by the time the fish was dead, all had faded to a dull brown. We also caught a large ray-fish, with its head the shape of that of an enormously large frog.

On some of these excursions we gathered a little sea-weed, which really deserves the name of sea-flowers, so beautiful are their forms. The coast, all along the sea-line, is very rocky and broken, and the surges come tumbling in from the sea in long, rolling, great ridges of water, which, dashing high up the rocks, have chiseled and fretted them out till some of them are almost as beautiful as a cathedral's "long drawn aisle and fretted vault."

On the 17th day of June, there came to me one of those days which come but once a year — a birth-day.

Brother and Sister Bardsley, with characteristic hos-
pitality and kindliness of heart, invited quite a little
company to spend the evening with them in their suburban home, and to make the time a very pleasant
one to me.   In every home I received a most kindly
welcome, and Brethren Kingsbury, Bardsley, Nelson,
Goode, West and Evans, each had their little home
tea-party, to put as much home sunshine into my life
as they could.

On the Wednesday evening prior to leaving, I gave
an address to all the young people connected with the
church and congregation, speaking from the words,
" Run, speak to that young man." " Teach the young
men to be sober."   " Teach the young women . . .
to be good."   I had a large congregation of young
people, and members of the church.   The attention
was so earnest and serious that we felt that abiding
good would surely result.   The same evening, as I
bade a long good-bye to Bro. Thos. Andrews and
wife and family, they put into my hand a little token
of their affection in the shape of a very beautiful
scrap-book, beautifully inscribed, and containing the
names of all.

On Thursday evening, June 23, the church held a
farewell tea-meeting, at which a goodly number sat
down to tea.   Then came the after meeting, presided
over by Bro. Hawkins, and very pleasing things were
said by the speakers selected for that hour.

On Friday, at noon, June 24, accompanied by Bro.
Strang and sixteen brethren and sisters, I went on

board, where we all took an affectionate leave of each
other, perhaps never to meet again on earth — they to
return to the busy affairs of this life, and to the cares
and struggles to be borne in the Master's work, and I
to set my face toward the far-off Nebraska home. At
noon the last hawser was cast off, and the strokes of
the engine, like the throbbings of a mighty heart,
told us we were already beginning our long voyage.
Hats were lifted, handkerchiefs were waved, and then
— as the gulf widened, and headland after headland
was passed, Sydney, and the friends who had come to
say good-bye, faded from view; and once more I was
alone.

Touching at Melbourne for about twenty hours, I
had the privilege of once more seeing my own
brother, with Bro. and Sister Haley, and a few
others. My brother, with also Brethren Haley and
Thurgood, accompanied me to the wharf. Bro. Thurgood is the brother, one of whose sons is now study-
ing for the work of the gospel in one of our American
universities. He is one who does a large amount of
good in a quiet way. The kindness shown to me by
him, and also by Brethren T. Magarey and P. Santo,
of Adelaide, was of no ordinary kind, and I would
write it here, but know that so doing would hardly
meet their approval.

Bidding them all farewell, I went on board once
more, leaving Melbourne at 4 P. M.; when in the face
of head-winds and heavy seas, we wended our way to
Adelaide. On the third day after, we dropped anchor

off Glenelg, in the Gulf of St. Vincent, a few miles
from Adelaide, and in sight of the beautiful home of
Bro. T. Magarey. I spent two hours on shore at
Adelaide, taking lunch at Bro. Gore's, himself not at
home — having gone to meet me, and missed me. His
good lady, the daughter of the Hon. P. Santo, made
me welcome with a kindness that was truly genuine.
On my return to the ship, I found both Brethren
Gore and T. Magarey waiting to see me, and to bid
me God-speed on the journey. Bro. Gore introduced
me to Capt. Dixon, the commander of the "John
Elder," who is also a Disciple, and a member of one
of the churches in Liverpool. Once more the warm
grasp of the hand, the kindly "farewell," and the
fervent "The Lord be with you," and these also
passed out of sight. It was a very pleasant thing to
hear Bro. Gore, Bro. Haley, and many others at every
point say, as they bade me farewell: " Bro. Exley,
we shall be glad to see you back again."

At noon, July 1st, we left Adelaide also, and were
soon again battling with the unabated storm, and
to add to our discomfort, although the bulwarks are,
I suppose, more than twenty feet above the water, the
waves seemed to find it *sport* to leap clean over them,
and send great sheets of foaming sea-water to the
very top of the smoke-stacks, and, after swirling and
rushing along the upper decks, to drip through and
through every crack to the saloon beneath, so that for
days a dry place was not the most easy thing to find.
Several times, I am told, off these Australian coasts,

the waves have dashed over the vessel in such volume
as to sweep all the cattle and every movable thing
overboard. I often found it a source of real pleasure
to watch the long-winged albatross scudding along
over the waves and between them, its long wings apparently now and then touching the water, and then,
rising high into the air, sail away, first one way and
then another, then round about in a great circle, but
to my sight scarcely ever waving a wing, though flying in the very teeth of the wind. As I thus watched
them, I thought of Dr. Bonar's beautiful words —

> " And these bright ocean birds, these billow rangers,
> These snowy-breasted, each a winged wave,
> These tell me how to joy in storm and danger,
> When surges whiten, or when whirlwinds rave."

I was hoping to be able to write something concerning the aborigines of New South Wales, and the
efforts that are being made by earnest Christian men
and women to protect and Christianize them, but the
documents promised me by Mr. Palmer, the Secretary
of the Society having these objects in view, were not
ready in time for me to receive them. I expect Mr.
Palmer to forward them to me to Nebraska. The
census returns, however, for South Australia, show a
total of 5,628 for that Territory, in 1881. Of these,
3,189 are males and 2,439 females. Since 1876 there
have been recorded 411 deaths and 301 births, making a net decrease of 110 in five years. Sickness is
prevalent among them to a great extent, no less than
959 adults, out of a total of 3,777, being unwell or

infirm. On the other hand, the children are not
numerous, the total number being only 892. The
end of this race does not appear to be far off. In the
other colonies they are diminishing at a still more
rapid rate. It is, however, a possible thing that the
efforts of good men and women to protect and Christianize what are left of them, may avert the extinction which now seems only too possible. I am
informed by my fellow-passenger, Rev. F. S. Poole,
that a fair measure of success has attended the efforts
of the Episcopalians, and that quite a number may be
considered as really redeemed men and women. With
others of them, however, little or nothing can be
done. From one or two newspaper leading articles I
saw, but failed to procure, if these were at all a fair
statement of facts, there can be no doubt but that
even now, in the vast territory of Queensland, the
most cruel wrongs are often inflicted on the natives.

JULY 16th. — Australia, New Zealand and Tasmania are very far from me as I write — lands of
marvelous resources, accomplishments and possibilities, all of them, and far exceeding any power of
mine to adequately set forth, yet still with the usual
drawbacks which seem to accompany human selfish-
ness, and enormous legislative blundering, as well as
some belonging to climate, soil and seasons.

On the night of July 10th we had the good fortune to see one of those very rare sights, a perfect
lunar rainbow. It is not easy to describe, being
about as like to the rainbow of the sun and the day,

as is the pale, dead face of a beautiful child, to the
light and joy and laughter and warm life-tints of that
face when living. Imagine a *dead rainbow* — all
there except its living glories; perfect in form, but
cold, ashy-colored, with the faintest touch possible of
the colors fled — and you have the lunar rainbow.

On the 20th of July we crossed the Equator, the
heat exceedingly oppressive, and nothing to break
the monotony. We are now fully 5,400 miles from
our last Australian port, Adelaide; but over all this
vast distance we have seen but one other vessel besides our own. How truly *great* is "the great and
wide sea!"

For the past few nights we have been favored with
what to us is a most welcome sight — the North Star
has become visible to us again, and we have the
splendid constellations of the *Great Bear* in the
North, and of the *Southern Cross* in the South, shin-
ing upon us at the same time. It is a very rest-giv-
ing thing here to remember that, " He knoweth their
number and calleth them all by their names — not
one faileth" — as if they were but so many sheep,
pasturing upon the blue fields of heaven, and that
vast as is this " great and wide sea." " He holds the
winds in His fists, and the waters in the hollow of
His hand."

On Friday, the 22nd of July, we sighted the first
land since leaving Australia — Cape Guardafui, Abys-
sinia; but the pleasure felt at the sight was almost destroyed by the high, hot winds, and the " no small

tempest" which "lay on us." Our voyage over the
Red Sea was full of the realest physical discomfort,
from first to last — either hot head-winds or none at
all, being the case the whole four days we were on it,
the water itself being eighty-eight degrees. Several
of our poor fellows were brought up from the stoke-
hole in a deadly swoon. One strong young man, a
passenger, volunteered to do duty for one of the men
for one watch, but at the end of four hours he was
brought up insensible. Mr. J. L. Young, a gentleman well·known to many of our brethren in Adelaide, and who, after spending about thirty years in
the Colonies, was returning to end his days in England, through the excessive heat, was smitten with an
apoplectic fit, and never rallied. Walking about on
the deck early in the morning — at 9 o'clock in the
evening we buried him in the Red Sea. It was very
impressive to hear the ship's bell toll out its solemn
funeral tones, as the moment of burial drew near.
The body was placed, after due preparation on a
board, with the feet out toward the sea, at the open
port of the after square, and covered with the ship's
ensign — its great red cross answering well to the
dead man's form. The captain and a large number of
the officers and passengers gathered around the scene.
The Episcopalian funeral service was tenderly and
impressively read by Mr. Poole. At the moment
when the body was about to be committed to the
deep, the low call of the boatswain's whistle was
heard, and the engines at once stood still; and as the

words, " We therefore commit his body to the deep,"
fell from the minister's lips, the body was gently
raised up by four strong servants of the ship, and
suffered to slide from beneath its red-cross covering
into the solemn waters beneath.   One short sound, as
of a "gulp," was heard, when he at once sank beneath
and beyond the action of the screw-propeller, the
sighing, sobbing sea shrouding him 'round, and all
was over. The boatswain's whistle again gave out its
subdued call, and in response our ship moved rapidly
on her way, leaving our friend to sleep in the waters
of the Red Sea until that time when "the sea shall
give up the dead which are in it." No flowers, placed
by gentle hands, will adorn his grave — only the
white foam of the crested billow,

" The daisy of the sea,"

and the hundred-fold beautiful

" Rainbow of the spray,"

flung there by the fingers of the sun, will beautify
his place of rest.

   On the 28th of July the distant peaks of Sinai
came into view, and remained visible for many hours.
To sail over the Red Sea, with the coast of Egypt
visible on the left and the lofty summit of Sinai visible on the right, is, to the believer, a very suggestive
thing.   Egypt, with its olden time civilization, its
cruel bondage ; the Red Sea, with its wonderful redemption for Israel ; Sinai, with its *law* " written and

engraven on stones," efficient to condemn, but not
efficient to pardon the transgressor — all spoke to me
of deliverance from the bondage of sin, of the Red
Sea of redeeming blood, and of our own personal
self-surrender to the leadership of our great Deliverer
and redeeming Lord ; when we, being "baptized into
Jesus Christ," were "baptized into his death," the
law of condemnation passed out of sight, and I joyfully exclaimed, "There is, therefore, now no condemnation to them who are in Christ Jesus; for the
law of the Spirit of life in Christ Jesus hath made
me free from the law of sin and death."

From our first sighting the coasts of both Asia and
Africa, until leaving them, nothing but a dreary desolation of rock and sand met our gaze — hundreds of
miles of unbroken desert, with lofty mountains far
back in the interior. The long belt of sand along the
entire line of the horizon, as the sun pours down
upon it his fierce rays, presents the illusive appearance of long golden stretches of a summer evening
sky just before the sun goes down, and the distant
mountains present the appearance of patches of cloud,
with lines and bands of light between. The illusion
is so perfect that it is difficult at times to feel sure
that it is all solid rock or shifting sand. Occasionally the white tents of some Arab encampment, as if
erected close to the sea, gave a pleasing variety to the
scene, and set us all wondering how they could live
in such a desert as that.

On our arrival at Suez, no sooner had we dropped

anchor than we were besieged by a fleet of small
boats, their Arab owners intent on trading and getting
gain. Merchants with feathers, robes, lace and small
wares, came on board. Hanging their boat-hooks on
any ledge the side of the ship offered them, they
pulled themselves up hand over hand, sticking their
shoeless toes against the smooth iron about as fearlessly as if they had found, cut out on purpose for
them, a flight of steps.

I had often read of Arab extortion, and so I
watched them with a tireless interest. Their eyes,
bright and restless, seemed to miss nothing; their
ceaseless chatter as they sought to sell their wares had
a charm for me that was fascinating, and so I wandered up and down the deck from one to another, to
see how these dark-skinned children of the desert
could manage to fleece the *honest* trading whites!
They will likely enough take advantage when they
have the chance; the very thing they very rarely get.
Extortion! I saw a large number of sales take place,
but whilst in every case the vendor was ready to take
a very large reduction from his own price, I did not
see one case where the original price asked was too
much, judging by trade transactions elsewhere. The
extortion was, as I thought, all on the side of the
whites. As a sample of Arab extortion, I saw fifteen
links of beautiful coral beads offered for seventy-two
cents; thirty-six cents was offered — and *taken*. No
wonder that they are nearly naked, and that Arab
beggars abound.

13

The journey through the Suez Canal, about ninety-three miles in length, was one hot torture during the whole twenty-four hours occupied in passing through it. The glaring sands on either side seemed to fling back at us the superheated rays of the sun, as if they delighted to torture. Occasionally the monotony was broken by groups of Arabs engaged in dredging or widening the canal; or a family of Arabs encamped on the burning sands, their camels laid down at rest.

On Saturday, the 30th of July, we reached Port Said, a city created by the canal, where we had the gratifying privilege of a few hours' run on shore. Port Said is a hard place. Blind beggars, crippled beggars, sick and creeping beggars, beggars young and old, lazy Arabs stretched out their full lengths on side-paths and other shady places — the streets filled with vendors of small wares, with here and there Egyptian women veiled from just below the eyes to the knees with a black veil, a chain of large gold or gilt rings passing down the center of the forehead to the nose, and each carrying a large water-jar on the head, in the most perfect equilibrium — all these, and other things, combined to produce a picture not soon or easily to be forgotten. To add to the charm of it all, one has but to reflect that he stands on Egyptian soil, or rather sand; and that the feet of Abraham, Isaac and Jacob, and Joseph and his brethren, may have pressed upon it; and over it, perhaps, have been driven many of the weary, suffering sons

of Israel, urged on under the blows of the task-
master's rod. Here again it seemed to me, that the
"extortion" practiced was by no means all on the
side of the Arabs. I was often asked for alms, but
never persistently. Once or twice "No," kindly but
firmly spoken, was sufficient.

At Port Said we took on board some 600 tons of
coal, every pound of which was put on by the Arabs,
with perhaps a few Nubians amongst them, the black-
est of all black men I ever saw, but tall, lithe and
straight as an arrow. This large quantity was all
lifted in about five hours. It was a strange sight to
me, to look upon these lightly built but wiry and
strong men, carrying such heavy burdens in rush
baskets on their backs between the shoulders, with a
rag wrapped 'round the head, the ends of it falling
behind so as to help to protect the neck and shoulders, and in many cases with only a shirt to protect
them, and in some scarcely that. They walked over
the rough coals under their heavy burdens in their
bare feet, and kept up an incessant clatter of
tongues. When any one had any instructions to give,
remark to make, or question to ask, it was always
done with the right hand stretched out.

There were two different tribes engaged on one
boat, not a wise arrangement at all; for if one of each
tribe got to blows, it was the signal for a general free
fight, and it was quite startling to witness the fierce-
ness with which they suddenly sprang upon each
other. This kind of pastime was indulged in two or

three times, which set me to thinking, that if anything like that was a common occurrence at the building of the Tower of Babel, no wonder they speedily left off and went their several ways.

A long and very heavy plank fell on the side of one of them, knocking him down, and apparently hurting him so much that it was with great difficulty he could rise to his feet again. I feared at first that his back was broken. Having got up again, he quietly folded his arms across his breast, with the hands on the shoulders, when another strong young man went behind him, put his arms around his neck, and grasping his hands firmly, then put his right knee against the injured one's back and gave him a severe wrench in the direction opposite to that inflicted by the falling plank. A rather curious piece of surgery, truly ; but the injured young man at once went to his heavy duty again. At Suez a goodly number of us bought the long-tasselled red Turkish *fez*, which, as a matter of course, we put on, and a red-headed lot we looked. Being exceedingly weary and far from well, I laid me down for a little while on the cushioned seats of the cabin, putting my *fez* on the table by my side. While thus resting, although it was not yet dinner time, mine was stolen.

As we steamed through the Suez Canal, Arabs sometimes ran along the bank, shouting for " backsheesh," with only a single garment on, and that held so as not to impede their running. It was on our arrival in Egyptian waters, we first heard the astound-

ing news of the attempted assassination of President
Gen. Garfield. The grief and consternation caused
by this intelligence was general all through the ship,
and the most fervent hopes and desires were expressed that he might speedily recover, and the crimi-
nal meet with a prompt retribution. At Naples the
first questions asked were all about the President.

At 5 P. M., July 30, we left Port Said and its half-
naked Arabs, and in a short time we were sailing over
the blue waters of the Mediterranean, with strong
head-winds, and oppressively warm. Capt. Dixon
was very kind to me, offering in the kindliest way any
little extra comfort the vessel afforded. He is a very
popular commander, and stands high in the estimation
of all. Passing by Candia, on Monday, Aug. 1, on
Thursday, the 4th, we had a kind of field day from
about 3 A. M. to 12 P. M., passing in review in that
time some of nature's grandest wonders. Shortly
after 3 A. M. I was up, and, first taking a bath, I hur-
ried on deck, and through the dull gray of the early
morning, saw the distant form of the mighty Ætna.

As the light broadened out, clouds of smoke or
steam were clearly seen to be issuing from its crater.
On the east it seems to slope away to the sea, but on
the west a large retinue of lofty lava mountains
stretch for a long distance, each one running in huge
ridges down into the sea; but every nook and corner
where a vine can grow seems to be turned to account,
and a large population is scattered all over these
almost inaccessible places.

Then came the Straits of Messina — Sicily on our left and Italy on our right, and both very close to us, for the straits are very narrow, and made narrower still to all unlawful rangers of the deep by strong forts and heavy ordnance to protect them. To assail Sicily or Italy at this narrow point, will demand a "striving" of no ordinary kind. As we sailed quietly between these beautiful shores, I thought of the "strait gate and narrow way that leadeth unto life." Not long after losing sight of the vine-clad slopes of Mount Ætna, Stromboli loomed up before us, volumes of smoke rising from its summit. On its western side an enormously wide and deep channel is visible, down which the rivers of lava have poured themselves into the sea. On the base of the northern slope some 1,200 people have their homes. Stromboli rises up out of the sea as one gigantic cone, as if disdaining fellowship with any besides, whilst away in the distance many other cones of huge proportions are scattered up and down.

As the evening closed in around us, the grand form of Vesuvius arrested all eyes, and although quiet now, the mountain is still giving signs of unextinguished fires. Pompeii and Herculaneum are each but a few miles away, and bear witness to its destructive energy. We were favored during the whole night in seeing on its topmost cone what to us looked like a magnificent "pillar of fire," and during all our stay, after the morning had come, a glorious "pillar of cloud by day." As we passed slowly up the Bay

of Naples, which is nearly seven miles in circumference, at nearly midnight there suddenly flashed upon
us from two vessels in the harbor, electric lights of a
most brilliant character. Whether done to give us
welcome or to show off the beauties of the city and
its entire surroundings, I know not, but as the lights
fell upon the Castle of St. Elmo, and slowly swept
over the city, the shipping and the bay, the effect was
indescribably beautiful. Everything seemed to be
bathed in a flood of strange light, not golden or
roseate at all, but a sort of weird compound of unutterable blue and green, and a brilliant mist of
dazzling white and purple tissue. I think that no
one of us who witnessed this will ever forget it.

Next morning, accompanied by a friend, I went on
shore for two hours. Of course, nothing worthy the
name of a visit was possible in that time ; but we lost
no time. Naples was before us, and we struck for the
center of the city. "See Naples and die," is often
written and spoken. All right, for those who wish to
do so, but I do not wish to die there. Seen from the
bay, with its Castle of St. Elmo on its lofty hight,
from whence, in revolutionary times, cannon have
sent shot into the city, and its palace and other public
buildings to the left, and far to the right its long line
of very handsome brick buildings, formerly used as a
granary, but now as barracks for troops — the domes
and towers which stud the city in all directions, the
palatial residences visible on the vine-clad hills behind the city, and stretching around the bay, with

smoke and fire-crowned Vesuvius towering over all
— thus seen, no pen can do it justice. Seen from the
inside of the city, the scene is changed indeed.
Theaters, churches, statuary, paintings, fountains,
grand as these all are, the streets are so *narrow*, the
houses so high — six, seven, and even eight stories;
the people can almost shake hands from opposite
sides — the crowds of poorly dressed, thin and care-
worn looking people, the close, unsavory atmosphere,
" Ichabod " will as well depict it as any other word.
We wandered the length of many streets, but the
most comfortable looking of all the people we met
were the crown-shaven or rope-girdled priests and
monks. We walked behind one of these well proportioned gentlemen, a priest or monk, around whose
ample throat was wound a collar — I suppose it once
was white, but now about the color of the *lava* sold
in the shops. We never saw a book-store, or the
semblance of one, except a shabby little book-stall in
one of the public open spaces, and seemingly with
nothing in it but songs and paper-covered volumes of
plays, nor did a single picturesque costume meet our
eyes. We were glad, indeed, to see Naples, even the
little we did, but having seen so much of it, I concluded that the best place in which to die, *is not there.*

The beggars of Naples are the most pertinacious,
the boldest and most insolent I ever saw. Young
girls thrust into my bosom small bouquets of flowers
and boxes of matches, and so adroitly that it was
difficult to get rid of them. Finding that we could

not be induced to give or buy, they turned away at last, wishing us a speedy journey to the place from whence they suppose Vesuvius draws his supplies. We had a whole tribe of small-ware merchants come on board. Extortionate enough they often were in their first charges, yet about as well checkmated by their customers as is at all desirable. It appeared to me, that it is with them as with the Arabs, the very small price obtained for anything they sell, must help to crush them down and make beggars of them all.

At 1 P. M., Aug. 4, we steamed out of the harbor, leaving its beautiful waters and the crowded city to those who shall come after, and in a short time we were outside, and Vesuvius, with its ceaseless pillars of fire and smoke, and this region of wonders were left behind. In a few days more we hope to be in England, from whence this will be posted to the *Standard.* One more letter, and, the Lord willing, I shall be HOME.   H. EXLEY.

OFF CAPE FINISTERRE, Aug. 9, 1881.

LETTER XVI.

BAY OF BISCAY, Aug. 10, 1881.

Leaving the Bay and City of Naples, as mentioned before, and utterly wearied with the long day's pleasure and ceaseless activity, I was glad to find relief and rest in sitting down to write.

On the third day after losing sight of Mount Vesuvius, on Lord's day evening, just before the sun went down, we were all delighted to get a glimpse of the bold Rock of Gibraltar. To unnautical eyes, distances at sea are very deceptive. Although our good ship was running according to the " log " about thirteen miles an hour, it was a long time after first sighting the famous " Rock " before we were close to it. Approached from the east, it presents a very close resemblance to a couchant lion, but by the time we were fairly abreast of it, the darkness of the evening had gathered around us, and instead of the grim fortress, with its instruments of death frowning upon us, the lights of one or two lighthouses flashed upon us, as out of benevolent eyes, their assurance of peace and safety.

The Bay of Biscay, of deservedly evil reputation in sailor song and story, though by no means calm,

(202)

was not severely stormy as we sailed over it, but just
rough enough to remind us that, notwithstanding the
bigness of our ship, we were after all "but a feeble
folk."

Mr. Plimsol, the merchant sailor, and the successful contender in the British Parliament for protection
to the sailor, asked of Sir Charles Adderly, the President of the Board of Trade, "what number of vessels had been lost in the Bay of Biscay since the
adoption of the 'load-line' act (Mr. Plimsol's measure), and what number in the corresponding period
preceding." Sir Charles Adderly replied that "from
February, 1874, to February, 1875, *before the adoption* of the 'load-line,' twenty-six steamers and 176
lives were lost in the Bay of Biscay; but from February, 1875, to February, 1876, since its adoption,
only two steamers and twenty-six lives were lost."
(*Engineer's Manual*, 1877.) There is much other
work for other Plimsols to do, before all the avoid-
able terrors of the sea are removed.

From Naples to London is about eight days' good
sailing—the monotony constantly broken by the appearance of ships bound to their several ports, and
the last two days by the letter writing to friends and
preparations to go on shore. A few hours before
touching at Plymouth, we were all delighted to see,
away off to our right, the Eddystone Lighthouse, a
splendid testimony both to the noblest benevolence
and to man's masterhood of the sea. From Plymouth, where we sent on shore a number of pas-

sengers and the mails, all the way up to Gravesend,
the scenery is very beautiful, and to us, who had seen
little else than the blue sea and the star-studded sky
for seven weeks, it suggested thoughts of "the beau-
teous land," and "the light that never was on sea or
shore;" and our thoroughly clean and newly painted
and well trimmed ship, safely now at home, gave very
lively hints to many of us of "the abundant entrance
into the everlasting kingdom," when the voyage of
life is safely over. As we passed up to our anchorage
ground, the waters literally alive with shipping, we
passed an American vessel of war, the Stars and
Stripes floating at her stern. I had never seen the
great flag look so beautiful before. I did not know
that I so deeply loved it till then, and almost in-
voluntarily I sprang to the side of the ship and
waved it a hearty "three cheers."

At noon, Saturday, Aug. 13, hiring a small boat,
and bidding the captain and a few friends "good-
bye," I left the John Elder, and in one hour was
rolling away on the cars from Gravesend to London,
where I arrived in time for a hearty welcome from
Bro. Black, who had come up from his sea-side visit
on purpose to meet me, Sister Black remaining there
with the younger members of the family. Bro. Black
is now retired from business, and as an elder in a
Christian Church, he has, so far as known to me, but
few equals. He is not only "apt to teach," but now
spends nearly as much time in actual *pastoral work*,
visiting the members of the church, as he formerly

devoted to business. He is an example to rich men,
such as I do not know another. Twenty years ago,
when laboring in London as an evangelist, his hospitable home was mine. *He generously sustained me
out of his own purse,* and took care that I was never
shabbily clothed. So freely, heartily, and lovingly
was this done, that although I was their guest this
way for several times and several months at a time,
after I left England and made my home in the Western States, I received from them a letter, telling me
that they never regretted my presence in their home
for a moment. Few, indeed, are the things that have
been sweeter to me in this life, than this. Years are
now whitening the heads of both Bro. and Sister
Black, but their hands do not slacken in the Master's
work, and, taken all in all, such loving, ceaseless,
self-sacrificing toilers, Bro. Black in the church, and
Sister Black in the Sunday-school, and in all good
works, I have never met in one church again. Surely,
their crown will be a crown of life.

I remained but some three days in London, visiting
in that time some of the faithful ones, whom, in years
long gone past, it was my privilege to help to find the
truth as it is in Jesus, and to baptize into the sacred
names. Amongst other visits, I went to see Bro. J.
B. Rotherham, with whom I had a most delightful
stroll, and chat about many things, along the Thames
embankment as far as the Cleopatra's Needle. Years
begin to tell on him; hard study and hard work and
much care are silvering his locks — whitening them

for the harvest-home. His New Testament is not half well enough known to the brethren in America; it corresponds very exactly in many of its renderings with the Revised Version. It will likely be found that in him Bro. Moore will have an able coadjutor in the most serious work he has ever undertaken — in seeking to plant a church in London.

From London I went at once to Southport, receiving a warm welcome from Brethren Moore and Garrison especially — the latter of whom I had never seen before. He is far from being strong, and the work on his hands is far from being free from care and anxiety. On the two Lord's days I spent in Southport, I preached for him, once in the morning and twice of an evening. Bro. Coop, I did not think was looking as well as when he left Adelaide in Australia.

During my stay in Southport, which was but a few days at intervals apart, it was my privilege to meet, in company at Bro. Coop's, Mr. Henry Varley, of London, whose evangelistic fame is known around the whole world. During some three hours, I think, with the open New Testament in our hands, and in company with an Episcopalian clergyman visiting at Bro. Coop's, we had a long and exceedingly interesting conversation as to the relations in which the law and the gospel mutually stood toward each other.

The deeply calm, reverent and earnest spirit of Mr. Varley takes one captive almost at once. Churches built up under such a ministry as his can not fail to be churches full of spiritual power. It may be that,

under God, such a man coöperating with Bro. Moore
in the double work of the pulpit and the press, if
faithful to the whole truth — compromising in nothing — these two will be enabled to inaugurate and
carry on the most glorious reformation work that
London and England have seen for many a day. The
brethren will *be justified in looking for large results.*

On Thursday evening, Sept. 1, the church at Southport held one of those, at all times, very pleasant
gatherings, a social tea-meeting, after which, Bro.
Garrison in the chair, several speeches were made,
when Bro. Coop, on behalf of the church, presented
a very beautiful time-piece to Bro. and Sister Moore.
The church in Southport grows but very slowly, and
at present is far from being a strong church — the difficulties which have lain in its path have neither been
few nor feeble. The congregations are thin, a result
of those difficulties ; and rich and deeply spiritual and
powerful as is the preaching of Bro. Garrison, it
will be slow work to carry the battle to a worthy
victory.

Bro. Garrison, as chairman of the meeting, referred
in touching terms to the wounded President, and
spoke of Mrs. Garfield in the most graceful manner
as "Our uncrowned Queen." The feeling in England toward President Garfield hardly ever had its
parallel. Men who were never in America, and never
expect to be, could scarcely utter his name without
tears in their eyes and a tremor in the voice. God
grant that the future may ever find that one heart and

soul may live and throb in both nations, as if they were but one people.

On Monday evening, Sept. 5, the newly planted church in Liverpool also had its tea-meeting — when quite a large company sat down to tea. Brethren Moore, Garrison, Van Horn, a Baptist minister, but whose name escapes me, with also Bro. Newington and myself were present. Bro. Garrison presided over the meeting. An address, beautifully illuminated and framed, and couched in terms which must have been very grateful to both Bro. and Sister Moore (for she was also present), was presented to them, on behalf of the Liverpool church, by Bro. Edmund Rowson, whom, with his excellent wife, it was my joy to baptize into the faith of Jesus when laboring at Birkenhead, a little more than a year and a half ago. Bro. and Sister Moore go to London rich in the affections of many. There are elements of real ability in the church at Liverpool — young men pious and devoted; but whether Bro. Moore has done a wise thing, so far as Liverpool is concerned, to go away to another field just at this particular time, the future alone can reveal. It may be seriously doubted. It was delightful to see so large a membership, and apparently all in real earnest and happy. I attended the services one Lord's day, presiding at the table in the morning, Bro. Newington speaking to the church, and my impression was that he will improve on acquaintance, for he spoke quite well, and without any notes.

In the evening, Bro. Van Horn, from Chester, was
the preacher. The large room was *well filled*, and
with an intelligent and earnestly listening audience.
Bro. Van Horn is a speaker of no mean order. I attended also a week evening meeting, and was very
much pleased to see such a goodly number of the
members present, many of them having come a rather
long distance to be there. Altogether, the work in
Liverpool appears to be good; but after all, we think·
it a mistake that Bro. Moore could not remain for a
few months longer.

On Wednesday, Sept. 7, bidding good-bye to Bro.
and Sister Moore, Bro. and Sister Coop, Sister Haigh,
and many others, accompanied by Bro. Garrison, I
left Southport, and at 4 P. M. was on board the steam-
ship "England," bound for the great Western land
once more. Old Father Cavan, one of the elders of
one of the Liverpool churches, and over eighty years
of age, came, having walked three miles to see me, to
say once more "farewell." Twenty years ago, all
unknown to himself, he gave me a lesson on preaching which has never been forgotten. Requested to
preach one evening during the sessions of the Annual meeting, by the desire of brethren in whose
judgment I had all confidence, I preached from the
words, "The weak things of the world," etc., putting
into the discourse quite as much of science as of
Christ. The wise old brother said to one who told
me his words, "Bro. Exley will never do for Liverpool!" Shortly afterwards, having to preach in the
14

same place again, the subject chosen was, " God mani-
fest in the flesh." The theme was *Christ* — from beginning to end, *Christ*. With tears in his eyes and
great earnestness in his manner, he spoke once more,
and said: " Bro. Exley is just the man for Liverpool!" Since then I have not ceased to teach and to
preach *Christ*. Bro. Cavan and old Bro. Corf, one
of the truest saints of earth, and also one of the
elders of the oldest church in Liverpool, are both
now nearly at the journey's end. The sweet intercourse of twenty years ago was renewed, and I visited
first with one, and then with the other. Both intensely Christ-loving, they, with Bro. Tickle, grudged
no toil or self-sacrifice, that His name might be
carried to the poorest and humblest. In all my own
work of tract distribution to thousands of homes, in
all my cottage preachings and out-door efforts to
spread the knowledge of the Saviour, they gave their
help and encouragement, like men who with all the
heart believed that the *name* of Jesus Christ was the
only bond and link between earth and heaven. It
was a very glad thing to know that much of the
fruit of that time abides in the Liverpool churches
to-day. There are densely populated streets where,
standing alone, and with by no means ungrudged per-
mission, on the door-steps of some cottage house, I
have read out a chapter, patiently waiting till a little
company had gathered around me, and then sought to
unfold to them the riches of redeeming grace. Once,
when thus engaged, a well dressed but badly intoxi-

cated man came, and taking his place just in front
of me, became very noisy and annoying. Deeply feeling the solemnity of my mission, I suddenly addressed him, and said, "Sir! I have a message from
God to you." He blundered out, "Well, what is
it?" I answered, "Drunkards shall not inherit the
kingdom of God." The effect was instantaneous —
he never opened his lips again, but stood to the
end of the service, and then quietly walked away.
Those days are gone now — days they were of hard
toil, of loving sympathy and earnest coöperation, and
of some fruit that still abides.

Bro. Newington's field of labor is far away removed from the other churches; they *might* coöperate,
but they are too remote from each other to unde-
signedly hinder.

Bro. Newington, Sister Rowson, and a few others,
came on board for a final *adieu;* and then, as our
ship, the "England," swung 'round to the turning of
the tide, the anchor was raised, and Liverpool quickly
faded away in the distance, perhaps never to be
visited by me again.

The voyage to New York was without special incident. We had a very large passenger list, of all
grades. It was very stormy at times, but to me quite
enjoyable. From Sydney, New South Wales, to London, and from London to New York, though often
unwell, sea-sickness was unknown. On the Friday
evening two days before landing in New York, a
ship's newspaper was started in our saloon, and never

before have I known how truly frivolous a number of
intelligent people can be when so disposed. On the
Saturday evening, by way of thanksgiving for our
safe voyage across the stormy Atlantic, a number of
them kept up song and dance until midnight. At
about 5:30 P. M., Lord's day, Sept. 18, I was safely·on
shore, being also met by Bro. William Neal, of Liverpool, whose father is a deacon in one of the Liverpool churches, and who came to the knowledge of the
truth under my labors there twenty years since.
Very shortly after, a very cordial Christian welcome
was given me by Bro. and Sister Carr, at whose
always hospitable home my stay was made for the
twenty-six hours I remained in New York. I was
fortunately in time to attend the special prayer-meeting appointed in the church, and, at ·the request of
Bro. Carr, gave a short address. A letter from
home urged me to lose no time, on account of the
serious sickness of ˙my wife, and so I took the
Monday evening train for the West, arriving at my
own home on Thursday evening, Sept. 22, just one
year and five days after leaving it, "not knowing
what should befall me." I found my dear wife very
sick indeed. She is better now. All the rest I
found well. I am led sometimes to think that more
strange providences, and mercies and struggles have
been mine than those of any one I have ever known,
and am often tempted to sketch out an autobiography,
with photographs of men and things in the churches,
with some others, as I have known them.

A few paragraphs more, and this letter will end the series, which, with all their faults, have consciously nothing extenuated,

"Nor set down aught in malice."

Bro. Coop and myself, wherever we went and whatever we saw, sought to go simply as Christian men, and to see, not as either Englishmen or Americans, but to see things as they were, and if we said anything concerning them, to say what was just and true. I could easily illustrate the evil that has been done, in more places than one, by drawing contrasts between England and America, with the tone, manner and matter disparaging to the former. The evil done is done quietly, but is almost incurable, and wherever done by a preacher, either one way or another, it proves a blighting influence on his work.

On the 17th of Sept., 1880, as my sons were cutting hay, about noon the sickle broke, compelling one of them to go to Lincoln to get it repaired. Had it not broken, he would not have gone. Had he not gone just when he did, or had the sickle broken on the previous day, this letter and all the rest, and all this strange and wonderful journey, would not have been. Breaking when the sickle did, it sent one of my sons to the Lincoln post-office, to find there for me the following telegram: "Meet me at Omaha to-morrow at 12 A. M. Take ticket for San Francisco, and I pay expenses.—T. Coop." After receiving it late in the evening, on hearing it read, my wife exclaimed:

"The Lord permitted that sickle to break just when it did." In about sixteen hours afterwards, I had packed my valise, taken an hour or two's sleep, traveled seven miles through storm and heavy roads to Lincoln, and some eighty miles to Omaha. Standing on the platform of the station at Omaha, Bro. Coop said: "Before we start, let us understand each other. How are we going? I pay expenses, and you——" "And I give my life and time and strength, free," was my response. And thus we started, each with the single-hearted desire that in some way the Lord would make it fruitful of good.

The soul of Bro. Coop may be clearly read in this: When fairly on the journey, I said: "Bro. Coop, you seem to me very much like the man in the gospels, as far as this journey is concerned — he began to build, you know, without counting the cost." He looked amused as well as thoughtful, and said: "*I* have n't counted the cost!" Bro. Exley responded: "But I *have*, and you can't take me this long journey, with all its incidental expenses, for less than about £300! That is a very large sum of money, and much as I love the idea of the journey, and especially of seeing Palestine, I do n't feel justified in allowing you to spend so much money on my account. I would much rather you sent me to Jersey Island to try and establish a mission there, and I will go and make it a *life work*, and £300 will go a long way toward fairly giving it a starting." After a moment's reflection, he said: "I do not care for the *money, if we only can do good."* We sought always and only to do good. If we failed, it was not the aim of either intention or effort.

As we voyaged between America and New Zealand, we made it a part of every morning's duty, and it was from the first a delightful privilege, to read together, chapter after chapter, the *Acts*, each making his own penciled notes, and then comparing them. Starting with the idea that the *Acts* reveal what was specially said and done under the immediate government of the Holy Spirit, and that it embraces the infallible history of the church for a period of over thirty years, we were struck with the fact that, nowhere, under any circumstances, is there such a thing as even a hint that Jesus had ever instructed his disciples, or that they had ever so understood him, that, the plenitude of the Holy Spirit and of power having come, and that full redemption being now accomplished through the one sacrifice on the Cross, they must therefore teach the people (the Jews) to forsake Moses, or cease to offer their accustomed sacrifices in the temple, or to abstain, *as Christians*, from anything commanded in the *law*. We noted that, had anything been said on the day of Pentecost that could by any possibility have been tortured by the " mockers," as against the law, the newly born Christian commonwealth could not have had *"favor with all the people."* We noted the facts of the third chapter, that Peter and John had no scruple against going up to the temple to participate in its solemn service at the hour of prayer, and that in his second sermon, Peter declared that Jesus had been sent to bless them, not in turning them away from *Moses and the law*, but "from their iniquities." We noted the fact that when arrested and brought before the Sanhedrim — that body of men so hungry for the overthrow of the Name — they were not charged with being in any sense teachers seeking to turn the people to a forsaking of the law, or the service it required; but "the priests, and the captain of the temple, and the Sadducees came upon them, being sore troubled, because they taught the people and proclaimed in Jesus the resurrection of the dead." Not less than 5,000 men in Jerusalem believe, but not one of them even suspects that the law is being set aside, and the Sanhedrim "let them go, finding nothing how they might punish them." We saw that *twice*, as recorded in the fifth chapter, were "the apostles" arrested, and put in prison or brought before the Council, but the only thing alleged against them was that they continued to teach in the forbidden *name*. All this being utterly beyond reasonable credibility, if the apostles had at any time taught one thing that would weaken the force of the law, or that such men, evidently watching how they might destroy the apostles, should have let them go, the more so as the apostles directly charged upon them the crucifixion of the Prince and Saviour, endorsed and sealed by the Holy Ghost. Nay, more: "*Every day in the temple*," as well as at home, they ceased not to teach and to preach Jesus

Christ. We wondered what certain modern "keepers of the temple," who talk about "the light that streams from the sanctuary," would say to the recorded fact that "*a great company of the priests became obedient to the faith,*" and of not one of them is it said that he forsook the law of his fathers, or gave up his customary service in or at the temple; nor even, if being of the class whose services consisted of singing in the temple choir, and of playing upon instruments of music, were they called upon to do such service no more. Here was "light streaming from the sanctuary" indeed; revealing such a gentleness in the gospel, and such large-hearted love in even the most "zealous for the law" adherents to the gospel, that no jar is felt in the church of *many thousands,* nor is there even a well grounded suspicion, in the mind of either believing or unbelieving Jew, that the law was being secretly or openly taught, or set aside, as of no further requirement to the Jew. Every attempt to fasten on the apostles, or any of the first proclaimers of the gospel, the charge of seeking to subvert the law of Moses, utterly fails. We also observed how that, with emphasis, James the apostle and the elders that were with him in Jerusalem, said to Paul: "Thou seest, brother, how many thousands (myriads) there are among the Jews which have believed; and they are all zealous for the law; and they have been informed concerning thee, that thou teachest all the Jews which are among the Gentiles to forsake Moses, telling them not to circumcise their children, neither to walk after their customs. We have four men which have a vow on them (*believers?*) These take and purify thyself with them, and be at charges for them, that they may shave their heads, *and all shall know that there is no truth* in the things whereof they accuse thee; but that thou thyself also walkest orderly, keeping the law" (R. V.). And Paul went and did it! We marveled that the Mother Church of all churches, under the very eyes of the apostles at Jerusalem, and under the very government and direction of the Holy Ghost, should at the end of thirty years after Pentecost, not have a man in it but who was " zealous for the law ;" and that the apostles themselves, with Paul also — Paul, the great preacher to the uncircumcision — should all be at special pains to show that all charges to the contrary were false. We saw that when Paul stood before Festus, charged by his countrymen with " many and grievous charges," he quietly said in his own defense, " Neither against the law of the Jews, nor against the temple, nor against Cæsar, have I sinned at all." We observed these and very many other facts and incidental statements, all showing such a toleration, gentleness and large-hearted charity as stand at an almost immeasurable distance from that zeal for the Lord's house which, with uncoverable bitterness, can ostracise and disfellowship all who do not conform, not to the gospel of Jesus, but to their dogmas concerning it. We saw that Paul never forsook the religion of his fathers, and that this was no bar to his

fullest communion with all who, in every place, called
upon the name of the Lord Jesus; and that his last
utterance on this matter, as given in the last chapter
of Acts, was, " I have done nothing against the people, or the customs of the fathers." From all this, we
concluded that the mission of the believer in Jesus
does not allow him, where unfortunately any breach
does exist amongst the brethren, to widen the breach
— to magnify any difference — to increase any bitterness, or misrepresent in any measure those from
whom he may differ. We gathered that, whilst the
believer must strive with all his heart to be loyal to
the Lord Jesus and his gospel, he must not, under
plea of faithfulness to the requirements of the gospel,
treat with unkindness, and place under ban any who
love the Master, but who have failed to gather up the
same measure of truth with himself. We thought we
saw a catholicity of spirit attending the proclamation
of the gospel, and filling its proclaimers, which always won the truth-loving, and never yielded or
compromised the gospel, even when with "all good
conscience" as Jews they forsook not the "law of
their fathers," and mingled in both the temple worship and synagogue service.

Occupied thus, day after day, our voyage was filled
from first to last with the realest interest, and we
think helped us to see men and things more nearly as
they really are, than we otherwise could have done.
Looking over the various fields of labor we visited, it
is but bare justice to say that the cause of a pure gos-

pel has taken deep root in all these far-off lands, and
that Brethren Earl, M. B. Green, of Dunedin; Gore,
Surber, Carr, Haley, Bates, Strang, Marston, with the
Australian preachers, have done no small share toward the present result. It may be also said that but
few preachers have ever had such faithful co-helpers
as they have found in the brethren themselves, without whose self-sacrificing hard work the labors of the
preachers would have counted for little. The *British
Millennial Harbinger*, published by the late Bro.
J. Wallis, of England, has had very large influence in
molding the character of the colonial churches, and
the *Ecclesiastical Observer*, Bro. D. King's paper, has
contributed in past years in the same direction. The
brethren in Australia have now, however, their own
papers, and conducted with real ability. Bro. Haley,
of Melbourne, is making the *Watchman* a power that
is felt.

Scattered over these vast Southern seas there are
still untamed lands and unredeemed peoples, and at
no great distance, India, China and Japan. Is it not
time that a common, loving effort be made by the
combined churches of America, England, and of these
Colonies, to carry the gospel to lands still benighted,
and "sitting in the darkness and in the valley of the
shadow of death"? Would it not be well for at least
one representative from the churches of Australia,
and one or two from Great Britain, to meet with the
brethren assembled at the next great annual gathering in America, so that some such work will be in-

augurated as will call out all our benevolence, absorb
all our energies, and swallow up all complaints, and
prove a starting-point from which shall be dated
the salvation of multitudes? The heart of the Australian brotherhood is large, and devises liberal
things. Their unstinted kindness to us, wherever we
went, will be sweet memories forever. Is it not the
duty of the present hour, that for united work for the
honor of Christ and the salvation of men, some effort
be made to gather together in one grand family feder-
ation and compact, all the children of God who are
scattered abroad?

On board the John Elder I preached three times;
on the voyage to New York it was too stormy the
only Lord's day it might have been possible.

The pen must now be laid aside; our long journey,
embracing the round world, with all its perils, has
come to an end; but its joys and pleasures belong
to the imperishable.

Wonderful indeed are the Colonies in these far-off
lands; wonderful is the work, it seemed to us, the
churches have there done; and wonderful the grand
possibilities and solemn responsibilities placed upon
us and before us a people. May we be found ready
for the work.

As Bro. Coop has really participated in all these
matters so much, it is only fitting that this letter
be signed in harmony with the first.

T. Coop, H. Exley.

October 27, 1881.